S0-DZF-003

BASEBALL'S
Hot New Stars

BILL GUTMAN

AN ARCHWAY PAPERBACK
Published by POCKET BOOKS
New York   London   Toronto   Sydney   Tokyo

AN ARCHWAY PAPERBACK *Original*

An Archway Paperback published by
POCKET BOOKS, a division of Simon & Schuster, Inc.
1230 Avenue of the Americas, New York, N.Y. 10020

ISBN: 0-671-65971-5

First Archway Paperback Printing April 1988

10 9 8 7 6 5 4 3 2 1

AN ARCHWAY PAPERBACK and colophon are
registered trademarks of Simon & Schuster, Inc.

Printed in the U.S.A.

IL 5+

THEY'RE YOUNG, TALENTED, AND ALREADY MAKING BASEBALL HISTORY

Who are your favorite major league stars? Never before have there been so many exciting young players, so many potential superstars playing at the same time.

The latest crop of young stars has surprised even veteran baseball fans. The talent on the field now is at one of its all-time highs. The hot new stars of major league baseball do it all—they hit, steal bases, field with Gold Glove ability, or hurl smoke. They are breaking records and bagging championships all over the diamond!

It's hard to pick only a few of the brightest stars. But here, in a collection any baseball fan will enjoy, are profiles of eight of the best. You will be amazed at what this talented group has accomplished in their short, shining careers!

Books by Bill Gutman

GREAT MOMENTS IN BASEBALL
GREAT MOMENTS IN PRO FOOTBALL
PRO FOOTBALL'S RECORD BREAKERS
REFRIGERATOR PERRY
STRANGE AND AMAZING BASEBALL STORIES
STRANGE AND AMAZING FOOTBALL STORIES
STRANGE AND AMAZING WRESTLING STORIES
BASEBALL'S RECORD BREAKERS
BASEBALL'S HOT NEW STARS

Available from ARCHWAY Paperbacks

Contents

BASEBALL'S
Hot New Stars

Don Mattingly *(Courtesy New York Yankees)*

Don Mattingly

Don Mattingly is at the top of his game. In fact, the first baseman of the New York Yankees is at the top of everyone's game. Since bursting upon the New York scene as a full-time player in 1984, Mattingly has won a batting title, has led the majors in RBIs, has been a Most Valuable Player, and has set a slew of league and team records.

In addition to this, he's been widely acknowledged as the best all-around player in the game by the best judges possible—his peers. In fact, in a 1987 statistical ranking of all major leaguers compiled by the Elias Sports Bureau, Don Mattingly received the first perfect score in the seven years the rankings have been kept.

What is it that Don Mattingly does that makes him so highly ranked and respected? The answer is everything. He hits for both average and power. He can drive the ball or punch it to the opposite field. He rarely strikes out. He is also steady in the clutch and a peerless first baseman who is a perennial Gold Glove winner.

Yet at the outset of the 1988 season, Don Mattingly will be just 26 years old. He is undoubtedly the hottest of baseball's hot new stars. But he didn't do it by numbers. He's also a ballplayer who has worked for everything he's achieved.

The Mattingly work ethic is already legendary. He can't get enough batting practice, working on each individual aspect of his hitting for hours on end. At first base he'll take ground balls by the dozen, practicing making his throws and fine-tuning his game again and again. He's being paid more than two million dollars a year for his efforts, but in the minds of most, if any ballplayer is worth that kind of money, it's Don Mattingly.

Yet Mattingly didn't join the Yankees organization with pomp and fanfare. On the contrary, he was a nineteenth-round draft choice out of Evansville Memorial High School in Indiana, a fine all-around athlete who had to prove himself in the minor leagues before making the leap to the bigs.

"I'm not flashy and I don't think of myself as a great player," Don Mattingly once said. "I think of myself more as an everyday player, a worker type. I want to be consistent. People will have to see my game over a long period to really appreciate it."

Don Mattingly was born in Evansville on April 20, 1962, the youngest of four brothers, all of whom were outstanding schoolboy athletes. In fact, one brother, Randy, played in the Canadian Football League for five years. Young Don learned quickly from his brothers, then began working his way through Little League, Babe Ruth League, and American Legion ball.

By the time he reached Evansville Memorial High, he was a three-sport star who was already working hard at improving himself. He expected to continue his career at the college level, and it's said that was the reason he wasn't picked earlier. But shortly after the Yanks picked him on the nineteenth round of the free agent draft in June of 1979, he signed.

He was joining a team steeped in tradition. The Yankees were perhaps the most well-known franchise in all of sports, a team that had won more pennants and World Series than anyone, the team of Ruth, Gehrig, DiMaggio, Mantle, Berra, Maris, and many other great stars. At first, that meant little to young Don Mattingly.

"Growing up in Indiana, you don't hear much about Yankee tradition," he admitted.

He began his Yankee career at Oneonta in 1979, playing in 53 games and hitting .349. He was mostly a singles hitter then. Among his 58 hits were 10 doubles, a pair of triples, three homers, and 31 RBIs. The next year at Greenboro in the South Atlantic League he began to make his presence felt.

Playing in 133 games, he led the league with a .358 average while switching between first base and the outfield. He also led the league with 177 hits. He had just nine home runs, though he did drive home 105 runs. At the age of 18, he was beginning to show the Yanks that they might have an up-and-coming player in their ranks.

After being named the South Atlantic League MVP, he moved on to Nashville in 1981, continuing his string of .300 seasons. This time he batted .314 with 172 hits. Yet he only managed seven homers this time, with 98 RBIs. So while he was moving rapidly through the minors, the Yanks did not view him as a potential power hitter. At 5'11", 175 pounds, they probably figured he was too small to consistently bang the ball out of the park.

In 1982 he was promoted to Columbus, the Yanks' top farm club, and he wailed away at a .315 pace, this time socking 10 homers and driving in 75 runs. He played the outfield most of the time, and in September was brought up to the big club for the traditional "cup of coffee," a quick look at the major leagues.

He had a pair of singles in 12 at-bats, then

wondered where he'd be playing in 1983. After winning the James P. Dawson Award as the top rookie in spring training the next year, he came north with the Yankees. Would he be playing in the bigs at age 21? He thought he'd have a real shot when he was named the opening-day first baseman.

Mattingly remembers. "I had three tough plays at first that day and none of them went my way."

Though none of the plays was ruled an error, and while he was one-for-three at the plate, he was immediately benched by then-manager Billy Martin. And on April 14, the 21-year-old was returned to Columbus.

"It wasn't so bad," Don said later. "I guess just about every big leaguer has a story like that. In a way it's good that it didn't come so easy. And I'll say this. The Yankees have never given me a thing."

But Don Mattingly never asked for favors, either. He returned to Columbus and went back to work. At that time he still described himself as a left-field hitter with an inside-out swing.

"I hit a lot like Rod Carew back then," he said. "I never tried to pull the ball, just put the barrel of the bat on it."

But he also began working with Lou Piniella about that time. Piniella was winding down his career as a player and doubling as batting coach. Lou began to work on having Don put more weight on his back leg. He wanted him to learn to drive the ball harder, turning on it and pulling it to right when the situation called for it. Under Piniella's tutelage, Don started becoming a complete hitter.

The Yanks recalled him in late June after he hit .340 during his tenure at Columbus, and he appeared in the majority of the team's games the rest of the way. When the season ended he had a .283 average in 91 games, with four homers and 32 RBIs. He was more determined than ever to make the club in 1984. He applied his work ethic once again, played winter ball in Puerto Rico, where he hit .368, and came to camp again in '84 ready to go.

Yogi Berra was the Yankee manager that year, as owner George Steinbrenner continued his game of musical managers. Berra told Mattingly that he would be a swing man, shifting between first base and the outfield. Don nodded, then sounded a warning.

"Once you get me in the lineup," he said, "you're gonna have trouble getting me out."

The prophecy proved true. Within just a week or so Mattingly was in the lineup on an everyday basis, and he proceeded to dazzle the baseball world in his first full season in the bigs.

He hit well over .300 for the year, but he also showed unexpected power, drove in runs, and played flawlessly at first base. Though the Detroit

Tigers were running away with the American League East race, Don Mattingly was establishing himself as a star of the future. And the future wasn't very far away.

As the season came down to its final day, both Mattingly and teammate Dave Winfield, the Yanks' acknowledged superstar, were battling for the American League batting title. All Don Mattingly did in that pressure-packed, clutch situation was get four hits in five trips to salt away the batting crown with a .343 average. That wasn't all he did in his first full season.

Not only did he become the first Yankee to win the batting title since Mickey Mantle in 1956, he also led the American League in hits with 207 and in doubles with 44. Where he really surprised people was in the power department. He had 23 home runs and 110 runs batted in. He had come from virtually nowhere to put together a superstar season. Now the question turned to consistency. Could he duplicate his numbers in '85, especially after the league's pitchers had a chance to see him more often?

What no one knew was that it didn't matter how many times the pitchers saw Don Mattingly. There was no weakness, no way to stop him on a consistent basis. Minor knee surgery set his spring training back, but once the season started, he was ready.

In the first half, he was merely good. He was

hitting over .300 again, but with only nine home runs in 337 at-bats. Maybe he wasn't a real power hitter after all, people thought. But in the second half he really exploded, slamming 26 home runs and batting .340 over the second half to finish the year with one of the greatest seasons in recent memory.

Though the Yanks were second to the Toronto Blue Jays in the A.L. East race, Don Mattingly captured the imagination of the baseball world. He wound up with a .324 average, had 211 hits, led the league with 48 doubles, belted 35 big home runs, and drove home a major-league-leading 145 runs. He also had 21 game-winning RBIs and won a Gold Glove for his fielding. And he struck out only 41 times in 652 at-bats. For his efforts, he was named the American League's Most Valuable Player.

"He had as good a year as anyone I've ever played with or against," said Lou Piniella, who would become Don's manager in 1986. "You knew the numbers would be good, but he made it look so easy that you didn't quite realize just how good they were."

Ron Guidry, the Yanks' longtime pitching ace, was also in awe of his young teammate.

"By the time his career is over," Guidry said, "he could be one of the best who ever played this game."

It wasn't only his teammates who praised him.

Players and managers around the league marveled at his skills and his work habits.

"I love watching him practice," said Angels manager Gene Mauch. "He's all business during infield practice and never wastes a swing in the batting cage. But once the game starts I don't want to look at him."

Carlton Fisk, veteran star of the White Sox, gave this evaluation of Mattingly after seeing him for just two years.

"He's the best in the league," Fisk said. "He hits for average, for power, and plays defense. Just the best."

And Don Baylor, another veteran who was both teammate and adversary, said, "If he made one dollar a year or two million, he'd be the same ballplayer with the same intensity."

Though he called it play, everyone knew that Don Mattingly was about the hardest-working player in baseball. The Yankees must have agreed when they signed him to a new pact, a one-year, 1.375-million-dollar deal for 1986.

It was to be another memorable year. The Yanks spent most of it chasing the Boston Red Sox, and Don Mattingly spent his time chasing records and Wade Boggs. Boggs was the Boston third baseman who seemed to be taking a lock on the A.L. batting crown. He had relinquished it to Mattingly in 1984, but reclaimed it in '85, and was leading again for most of 1986.

Mattingly the hitter is perhaps the most dangerous
man in baseball. He can go to the opposite field, or
he can pull the ball into the seats. *(Courtesy New
York Yankees)*

As usual, Don Mattingly was having a great season, and he seemed to get even better as the year wore on. The Red Sox had sewn up the A.L. East but had to meet the Yanks in a final, four-game set. Going in, Boggs was batting .357 and Mattingly was at .350. But Boggs had a slight hamstring pull and the Sox announced he would sit out the four games with the Yanks so he could be ready for the playoffs and perhaps the World Series.

Mattingly fans howled in protest. They said Boggs was avoiding a direct confrontation with Mattingly for the A.L. bat crown. A New York paper had the headline CHICKENED OUT in reference to Boggs missing the four games. Mattingly was quick to issue a disclaimer for the stories.

"If you read one quote that even hints at my questioning your injury, don't believe it," he told Boggs. "If I were hurting and had the playoffs to think about, I'd do the same thing."

Don then went out and had an eight-for-19 series against the Bosox, raising his average to a final .352. He hit a number of other balls right on the button that were caught. It was quite a show, one that even had the partisan Red Sox fans cheering. Though he didn't win the batting title, he was now unanimously acclaimed as the best player in baseball.

It had been an amazing year, with the highlights too numerous to mention. He had 31 homers and

113 RBIs to go with his .352 batting average. His 238 hits broke the all-time Yankee mark of 231 set years earlier by Earle Combs, and his 53 doubles cracked another Bomber standard, the 52 set by the immortal Lou Gehrig back in 1927. He also became the first American Leaguer ever to get 230 hits, 30 home runs, and 100 RBIs in the same year. He even filled in at third base for several games. A left-handed third baseman in baseball is a rarity, but Mattingly played the position flawlessly. And he won another Gold Glove for his play at first.

To make his run at Boggs possible, he hit a smoking .422 in the month of September. It was impossible to say a negative thing about him. As Yankee Coach Jeff Torborg put it:

"Once again he led the majors in character."

Before 1987 began, Don Mattingly made news once more. When he and Steinbrenner couldn't agree on a contract, he went to arbitration and won a whopping $1,975,000 salary for the year. He was nearly a two-million-dollar man.

It was to be an unusual year for both Mattingly and the Yanks. This time the Bombers led the division for much of the year, before injuries and a pitching collapse took their toll. The biggest injury was to Rickey Henderson, the speedy leadoff man who means so much to the team. Henderson had a stubborn hamstring injury that kept him either on the bench or at half speed, and that hurt.

As for Don, he started slowly, mired in a strange slump for the first part of the season. On May 15, he was hitting an anemic .240, claiming he just didn't feel comfortable at the plate. He was just starting to pick up the pace in early June when he felt sharp pain in his back. The diagnosis was a pair of damaged disks, and for the first time in his career he was placed on the disabled list.

When he went on the shelf, Mattingly had a 15-game hitting streak, during which time he was 24-for-55 for a .455 mark. His season's average was up to .311 with six homers and 36 RBIs. It was extremely frustrating for him to be injured, and when he finally returned toward the end of June, he was still hot.

On July 7 he cracked a pair of homers in a game against the Twins. A day later he hit one against the White Sox. The day after that it was a grand slam and the next day another solo shot. When he smacked another solo blast off Sox pitching on July 12, it marked the fifth straight game in which he had homered. The record for that feat was eight, set by Dale Long of the Pirates back in 1956.

The Yanks moved on to Texas and, boom, Mattingly did it again, blasting a pair. The next day he hit another for his seventh straight. With a chance to tie the 31-year-old record, Mattingly just missed a homer his first time up. But in the fourth inning against José Guzman, he did it, blasting a shot into the right-field stands for his eighth straight.

"After my first hit was so close but didn't go out, I didn't think I'd hit one tonight," he said after the game. "I've been on streaks before, but this one's ridiculous."

The next night, with a chance to break the mark, the streak ended. Tying the record, however, had been an achievement in itself.

"I never really felt any pressure through this whole thing," Don said. "I knew it would end one way or the other, and while I was trying to hit one, there was no disappointment at all."

Shortly after tying the record, however, Mattingly missed several games with a sprained wrist. Perhaps he had been trying too hard to break the mark, causing a slight injury to become even more aggravated.

The wrist injury bothered Don for a while, and what made matters worse was that the Yanks slowly dropped out of the race once again, as Toronto and Detroit battled for the A.L. East title. Yet before the season ended, Mattingly came back to set still another all-time mark.

Prior to 1987, Mattingly had never hit a grand slam home run. That year, he seemed to hit one every time he came up with the sacks full. By mid-

September he had tied the all-time mark with five. Then on the night of September 29, he came up again with the sacks jammed in a game against the Red Sox at Yankee Stadium. Facing lefty Bruce Hurst, Mattingly got his pitch and pulled it into the right-field stands for his sixth slam of the year. A new record.

"This felt good," he said afterward. "It's good to do something nobody's done before. But I wish Winnie would have hit it. He needed the four RBIs more than I did."

Mattingly was referring to teammate Dave Winfield, who was trying for 100 RBIs for the sixth straight season. Who said Don wasn't a team player?

When the season ended, the Yanks had dropped to an embarrassing fourth-place finish. But despite missing time to injury, Don Mattingly had put together another fine season. He finished with a .327 batting average, 30 home runs, and 115 ribbys. Because he had missed some 20-odd games to injury, he failed to get 200 hits for the fourth year in a row, finishing with 186. But very few people questioned his place at the top of his profession.

The question now seems to be just how far Don Mattingly will go. If he stays healthy, his numbers will definitely put him up with the all-time greats, and earn him a ticket to the Hall of Fame after his playing days end. Toward season's end, even

Yankee boss George Steinbrenner was praising his first baseman as one of the very best in the game. And both men have the immediate goal of getting the Yanks back to the World Series where they have been so many times before.

But no matter what, Don Mattingly will remain the same hardworking player he has always been.

"I want to improve every day and in every facet of the game," he once said. "Only when I feel I'm prepared for a game can I relax and have fun. There are tons of players who could be a lot better than they are. In fact, I'd like to have some of the talent of those guys. Give me their talent and I'll do some really big things."

Now that, coming from Don Mattingly, would really be something to see.

Eric Davis

Whenever an exciting young ballplayer comes into the major leagues, someone inevitably plays the comparison game. They'll compare the youngster to a superstar of the past whom he might resemble in style or looks—but not yet in talent.

While the younger player might have the potential to someday rival the legend, he's got to prove himself on the field. Whether or not he fulfills his promise is a question that only time will answer. While making comparisons might be fun, they can pressure a young player, and added pressure can have an adverse effect on his performance.

Take the case of Eric Davis, the fleet-footed center fielder of the Cincinnati Reds. Davis's natural skills enable him to hit for average, hit with power, steal bases, run, throw, and field brilliantly,

Eric Davis *(Courtesy Cincinnati Reds)*

and thus he was almost instantly dubbed the next Willie Mays.

Mays, known as the Say Hey Kid, was the most exciting and arguably the best player of his generation. He had all the natural skills attributed to Eric Davis, and put them to use during a Hall of Fame career that began with the old New York Giants in 1951 and ended with the New York Mets in 1973.

Among Mays's many accomplishments were a .300 lifetime batting average, more than 3,000 career hits, and 660 home runs, good for third place behind Henry Aaron and Babe Ruth. In addition, Mays made one electrifying catch after another, and is remembered especially for the one he made in the 1954 World Series, when he went into the far reaches of the old Polo Grounds in New York to rob Cleveland's Vic Wertz. That one's a classic.

Now how can someone honestly call a young ballplayer like Eric Davis the next Willie Mays? It isn't really fair, but such comparisons have been a baseball reality since the beginning.

"Eric Davis can do anything he wants in a baseball uniform," said his manager, Pete Rose, who should know something about ballplayers since he has more base hits than any other player in the history of the game. "He's the one guy who can lead our league in both home runs and stolen bases. Name another cleanup hitter who can steal 100 bases."

Consider the words of Davis's then teammate and veteran superstar Dave Parker, another big booster of the younger man's talents.

"Eric has tremendous bat speed and power, world-class speed, great leaping ability, and the body to play into his forties," Parker said. "He also has a throwing arm you wouldn't believe. There's just an aura to everything he does. I tell you frankly that I'd pay to see him if I had to."

Or this from Los Angeles Dodger manager Tom Lasorda. "The guy can hit 50 home runs and steal 100 bases in a season. I guess the last guy you could say things like that about was Willie Mays."

So there it is again. And all this was said about a youngster who had completed just one full season in the majors—a season that was somewhat clouded by a series of nagging injuries. Yet Eric Davis has heard the comparisons and he doesn't really care for them.

"I'm being compared to the impossible," he has said. "I've got a long way to go before people can say something like that. And to tell the truth, I never saw Mays, Hank Aaron, or Roberto Clemente. Why not compare me to my peers, guys I play against every day like Tim Raines, or Don Mattingly in the American League? Compare me to them."

Whether you compare Eric Davis to players from the past or those of the present, one thing is certain. He is one of the finest young ballplayers of his generation, and a player who has a definite chance to put up Hall of Fame numbers before his playing days end.

In fact, Davis's 1987 season was somewhat deceiving. He wound up the year with a .293 batting average, 37 home runs, and 100 RBIs, numbers most players dream about. But before a series of injuries slowed him, he was headed for a super year.

For instance, by mid-May, Eric Davis was hitting .358, had already belted 15 homers, and had driven in 38 runs. Project those figures over a full season, and Davis would have had 66 homers and 166 RBIs to go with his .358 average. And with the potential for that kind of production, no wonder people call him the next Willie Mays.

But while Eric Davis was only 24 years old at the beginning of the 1987 season, his rise to National League stardom hadn't come overnight. He signed with the Reds right out of Fremont High School in Los Angeles in 1980, and made his minor league debut that same year in Eugene, Oregon, at the age of 17. With several seasons in the minors, he paid his dues.

It all began for Eric on May 29, 1962. He was born in Los Angeles, the son of Jimmy and Shirley Davis, who had come to California from Mississippi two years earlier. Young Eric grew up in a rough neighborhood where it wasn't difficult for a kid to find trouble. Instead, Eric found sports.

Jimmy Davis always encouraged his son's athletic skills, even to the point of sometimes trying to arrange for him to play in other neighborhoods. He wanted to put him in a different Little League from the one in which Eric played, but couldn't because the family didn't live in the neighborhood. And later, he even wanted to have Eric bused to a high school in the suburbs. But that didn't work out, either, and Jimmy Davis later admitted it was for the best.

"All I wanted was for Eric to have use of the best equipment and play on the best fields," Jimmy Davis explained. "But as it turned out, staying in the neighborhood was the best thing for him. He had good friends, the competition was really fierce, and the kids were tough. Living here prepared him well."

When Eric entered Fremont High, he was already a fine all-around athlete. And he'd be going to a school that had already produced a number of major league baseball players, including Bobby Tolan, Bob Watson, George Hendrick, and Chet Lemon. Yet when the coaches saw Eric's slim and trim build, they felt he was better suited to basketball.

"The first day of baseball practice they sent me home, because they felt I was just a basketball player," Eric related. "But my father wouldn't hear of that and insisted I go back out. Two days later I had my uniform."

It didn't take Eric long to become a star in both baseball and basketball. He played point guard on the hardwood and shortstop on the diamond. And he soon began making a name for himself. Moreover, Eric believes that sports were a big reason he never got into trouble.

"When I look back I realize it was really a matter of survival in that neighborhood. There were street gangs and drugs, all of the things that can burn you. But I was so involved with sports I never had time to join a street gang, even if I wanted to."

Eric began to make friends within the sports world. One of his new friends was a ballplayer for rival Crenshaw High named Darryl Strawberry, now a star with the New York Mets. Strawberry was a year ahead of Davis and an outstanding player, but many felt Eric was just as good. Yet Strawberry received a wealth of publicity in high school and even had an article written about him in *Sports Illustrated* magazine. So it came as no surprise that he was baseball's number-one draft choice in 1979.

There were those who felt, however, that Davis didn't get the same kind of publicity because Fremont High was in a tougher neighborhood than Crenshaw, and not too many scouts would venture in to look at the players. One who did, though, was Larry Burton, Jr., who worked for the Cincinnati Reds.

"Yeah, there were scouts who had their problems over there," Burton admitted. "Stuff like slashed tires and broken windshields. But I got friendly with the baseball coach, who was a big guy nobody messed with. And through him I got to know Eric.

"He already had great bat speed and was really in control out there. I remember him stealing both second and third a number of times and not even bothering to slide—he was that quick."

By his senior year Eric was already an acknowledged star. He was the league's MVP and also all–Los Angeles in both baseball and basketball. On the court, Eric was the second highest scorer in the league, a slick point guard who could do it all. And on the diamond—well, all he did was hit .635 and steal an amazing 50 bases in just 19 games. That's 50 steals in 50 attempts. He wasn't thrown out once, not a single time.

There were already people interested. The Dodgers gave him a tryout, and one of their scouts told Eric they wanted him. As it turned out, they didn't. Same with the Milwaukee Brewers. Only Larry Burton and the Reds remained interested.

At the same time, Eric was getting feelers from a number of colleges. It was said that he could have had full baseball/basketball scholarships to at least three major universities—Arizona, Arizona State, and Pepperdine. Although by then, Eric Davis was thinking basketball, when the Reds made him just their eighth choice in the June 1980 draft, he was interested.

"I decided to give baseball a year or two," Eric said. "I figured if it didn't work out I could always return to college."

So he signed with the Reds for the very modest sum of $18,000, and reported to Eugene, Oregon, in the Northwest League. And for the first year or so, he thought he had made a mistake. His early years in the minors were not happy ones.

"A lot of the things that happened that year were negative," Eric recalled. "One instructor told me to just try to beat the ball down, that I'd never be a home-run hitter. It was as if they were telling me I couldn't achieve the things I wanted. To tell the truth, I almost quit."

Eric hit only .219 in 33 games at Eugene that year, with just a single homer and 11 runs batted in. He was still playing shortstop then, but his thoughts were moving toward basketball, or maybe college. It was his father, once more, who gave him the encouragement he needed.

"I told him to stick it out," Jimmy Davis said, "that maybe they were trying to test him. I said he couldn't let anything stop him, that God had given him all that ability and it wasn't meant to be taken away."

So Eric returned to Eugene in 1981. He wasn't

yet 19 years old, but he slowly began to make his mark in the Reds organization. He batted .322 that year, as the Eugene team began using him more often in the outfield. He also managed 11 homers and 39 RBIs, as well as a league-leading 40 stolen bases in just 62 games. Thoughts of a basketball career were fading fast.

After being named team MVP in Eugene, Eric moved to Cedar Rapids in 1982, where he hit .276 and swiped another 53 sacks. His 1983 season was split between Waterbury and Indianapolis, as Eric continued to play well and improve. He definitely seemed ticketed for the majors. The only question was when.

Eric started the 1984 season in Wichita. He was hitting over .300 when he finally got the call to join the parent club in midseason. Though he was an outfielder now, the Reds still envisioned him as a speedy leadoff man, who would get on base and steal a lot of bases. In other words, his job was to set things up for the power men further down the lineup. It was soon obvious that the strategy wasn't working.

In 174 at bats with the Reds in 1984, Eric hit just .224 and struck out 48 times. He did manage 10 homers and 30 runs batted in, but surprisingly swiped just 10 bases. Not the stuff future superstars are made of . . . except for one thing.

During one four-game stretch in September, Eric blasted five home runs, becoming the first

Cincy player to hit home runs in four straight games since George Foster in 1978. There was that awesome potential, visible for the first time to Cincinnati fans. Maybe they did have something more than a speedy leadoff man coming to the club.

Many thought Eric would become a regular outfielder in 1985, but when he struck out 31 times in his first 90 at-bats, he was promptly sent back to the minors. Was he now another young phenom about to fizzle? Veteran coach Billy De-Mars, the Reds' hitting instructor, didn't think so. But he did see a flaw in young Eric's batting style.

"He had the bat wrapped up in back of his head," DeMars said. "He could get away with it in the minors, but against major league pitching he simply couldn't get the bat head out in front fast enough."

At first Eric didn't see that as the problem. He thought it was a matter of pressure, and being in the wrong spot in the lineup.

"Leading off in the minors, no one ever told me to hit the ball on the ground or bunt. I was never a guy to choke up and just punch the ball."

So Eric played most of the season at Denver, but returned to the Reds late in the '85 campaign. And this time he began working with DeMars almost every day. By the time 1986 rolled around, he was ready for the big leagues.

"My swing was the same," he said, "but I

Thin but strong, Eric Davis has a quick bat and a powerful swing. His combination of speed and power makes him perhaps the next great all-around player in the game. He does everything well. *(Courtesy Cincinnati Reds)*

lowered my hands down in front more and took a shorter stride, so my bat was coming through a lot faster. Plus they dropped me down in the order, so I didn't have to worry about setting the table for the big guys. Instead I could relax and just try to hit the ball as hard as I could."

What Eric didn't say was that he was quickly becoming one of those big guys. It didn't happen in April. He started slowly, even with the new stance, and after hitting just .185 the first month, he found himself on the bench for much of May and he undoubtedly feared another trip to the minors. But in June his fortunes began to change.

It began with an injury to Nick Esasky, paving the way for Eric's return to the lineup on an every-day basis. His average was just .214 when he got his shot, but it didn't stay there for long. And National League pitchers quickly discovered they had a new force to contend with.

In June that year, he hit .361. Then in July he really exploded, batting a cool .381 with six homers, 16 RBIs, and 25 steals in 26 tries. For his efforts, he was named National League Player of the Month. Eric Davis had finally arrived. It might have seemed a long odyssey—his five-year trip through the minors, with two previous tries with the parent club. Yet Eric Davis was still only 24 years old.

He continued to play exciting baseball. In July he also put together a 17-game hitting streak.

Later he tied three club records, and on September 10, he belted three home runs in a single game against the San Francisco Giants. In another seven-game stretch, this one during August, he hit .462 with five homers and 16 RBIs. He showed himself to be the kind of ballplayer who could carry an entire team on his shoulders.

When the season ended, Eric was clearly a coming star of the game. He wound up with a .277 batting average, 27 home runs, and 71 runs batted in. In addition, he had stolen 80 bases, joining the Yankees' Rickey Henderson as the only players in baseball history to hit more than 20 homers and steal 80 or more bases in a single season.

And he did all this after his horrendous start, while he played in just 132 of the team's 162 games. He was also still a player without a position, having started 62 games in center, 42 in left, and 5 in right field. But Cincy plans called for him to be the starting center fielder in '87.

Now big things were predicted for him. In the offseason, Eric kept in shape by playing some basketball. He hadn't lost his old skills, scoring an incredible 49 points in a benefit game in San Diego with other baseball stars, including Tony Gwynn of the Padres, Darryl Strawberry, and Chris Brown of the Giants.

And every week Eric, Strawberry, and Brown, another L.A. native, would go back to Harvard Park, near where Eric grew up. There, they would

take turns pitching to each other and belting baseballs high and wide as the neighborhood kids
scurried to retrieve them.

"We've all moved away now," Eric said, "but
going back there serves as a reminder of how it
was and makes me that much more determined to
work hard and do well. It kind of gives me an edge
I need to stay on top of things, deal with the
pressures. I guess you could say it keeps me fired
up."

The Reds felt they would have a contending
team in 1987, especially if the pitching held up.
Eric was expected to approach or reach superstar
status, and big Dave Parker was still a force to be
reckoned with. The team also had other promising
youngsters, such as Kal Daniels and Tracy Jones,
as well as young veteran Nick Esasky. Veterans
Buddy Bell and Bo Diaz added stability. In fact,
the team looked so strong that the great Pete Rose
decided to keep himself off the active roster and
stick only to managing.

As predicted by so many, Eric started the season on a batting, running, and fielding tear, and
showed no signs of slowing down. That's when the
comparisons to Willie Mays really started, as
everyone in baseball was singing the praises of
Eric Davis. He was doing everything that had
been predicted of him—hitting for average and for
power, stealing bases, and using his great speed
and leaping ability to cover center field like a

blanket. Nothing seemed to get past or over him. In fact, he even robbed his old pal Strawberry of a home run with a leaping grab at the fence.

By the first week in May he was hitting a league-leading .411, with 12 homers and 27 RBIs. And he was coming off a weekend in Philadelphia that players and fans wouldn't forget for a long time. Against the Phils, Eric went 9 for 13 with five home runs and 11 ribbys. Incredibly, two of his homers were grand slams. And the season was just 25 games old.

"He's got the quickest hands I've seen in all my years around this game," said coach Billy De-Mars. "He's got to have great strength to be that quick."

According to Eric, bat speed was a necessary ingredient of his success.

"I'm not a real big guy," he said, "so I have to generate bat speed to hit the ball hard. To tell the truth, I really think that all the years of dribbling a basketball helped to build up my hands and wrists."

Whatever it was, it was working. Even the grizzled Pete Rose was impressed with Eric, and Rose had seen a lot of the best ones during his long tenure in the game.

"I'm not going to be surprised by anything he does or any standards he sets," Rose said. "It's really up to him now to be as good a player as he wants to be."

But there was one word of warning, and it came from an unlikely source. Davey Johnson, manager of the rival New York Mets, had this to say.

"Everyone is jumping the gun on Eric Davis," Johnson said. "And it's not fair to him. When people lead you to believe you're that good before you really are, it's an albatross around your neck. Let him improve on his own and just enjoy the game. Otherwise the pressure can be too great."

Maybe Johnson had a point. For there would be down times. The week before his batting tear in Philly, for instance, Eric had struck out nine straight times in a pair of extra-inning games to set a record. Yet by the end of May he had set still another record by hitting 19 home runs the first two months of the season.

But shortly after that his problems started, problems that no ballplayer can totally control. He began running into injuries. The first occurred when he made a sensational, diving catch on a ball hit by the Cards' Terry Pendleton. The bases were loaded with one out, and Eric didn't want to let the ball fall. He came up throwing, but also came up with a deep shoulder bruise and had to leave the game.

Then before the all-star break he injured an ankle, an injury that would rob him of precious speed and mobility. And while he missed very few games, he was suddenly operating at something less than full speed.

33

"It's the way Eric plays," Manager Rose said. "He goes all out and he's going to have bumps and bruises, wear and tear."

Eric was an all-star in '87 and his numbers continued to be up with the leaders. But after his meteoric start, the injuries had brought him back to earth. The hurt shoulder might have been responsible for a four-for-45 slump in June. And in the second half, as the ankle injury continued to slow him down, the Reds pitching faltered and the team slowly dropped out of the pennant chase.

The final blow came on September 4, when Eric once again made a game-saving, spectacular catch. This one occurred in Chicago, and he ran into the ivy-covered brick wall at old Wrigley Field. The result was a painful rib injury that kept him out of 16 of the Reds' final 27 games. And when he did play he was relatively ineffective, getting just five hits in his final 32 at-bats.

It was that final injury that took much of the luster from what could have been a banner season. Even with his problems, Eric finished at .293, with 37 homers and 100 RBIs. But he didn't approach his 80 steals of the year before and injuries were the reason.

So in a sense, the jury is still out, and the word "potential" still hovers over Eric Davis. There is no doubt about his natural skills. They're at or above superstar standards. But there have been ballplayers with those skills whose entire careers have been damaged by injuries. Pete Reiser was one, Tony Oliva another.

And maybe Davey Johnson was right. Maybe all the praise came too soon and the pressure was a bit much to bear. But Eric seems to handle it. It will take a season of good health for Eric to really show what he can do. As for now, he, too, would like to see the comparisons stop.

"I don't even know myself what I can ultimately do in this game," he has said. "Maybe I won't know until I'm done. But I know I'm not the next Willie Mays. I just want to be the first Eric Davis."

Kirby Puckett

One of the most famous quotes in the long history of baseball was uttered by the legendary Leo Durocher. Leo the Lip, known for his competitiveness and no-quarter attitude during his tenure as both player and manager, is often quoted as having said:

"Nice guys finish last."

But, like many striking remarks, the truth of Durocher's quote really depends on the situation and the talent. A nice guy with little or no talent may well finish last, or close to it. But a player of great talent, who also happens to be a nice guy, is going to be a winner. That's a fact. And here's an example.

His name is Kirby Puckett and he's the center fielder for the world champion Minnesota Twins.

Kirby Puckett *(Courtesy Minnesota Twins)*

To his teammates and others who know him well, Kirby Puckett is one of baseball's nice guys, a man who thoroughly enjoys his work, doesn't threaten his way to every last dollar, loves his teammates and the city in which he plays, and never brags about his own considerable achievements.

Puckett is a baseball rarity in more ways than one. Standing just 5' 8" and weighing some 210 pounds, he appears stocky to some, downright fat to others. But he's neither. He may well be the strongest man in baseball, able to generate tremendous power at home plate.

He's also extremely fast, and covers center field at the enclosed Metrodome, or at any other ballpark, like a blanket, often robbing opposing hitters of extra-base hits and home runs. In some ways he is reminiscent of the great Ernie Banks, a Hall of Famer but also a man who always played the game for fun.

"Baseball was fun for me when I was a kid," Kirby Puckett has said, "and it's fun now. I just love the game."

And the game is just beginning to love Kirby Puckett. For his kind of enthusiasm is contagious, and he's become the spirit of a team that surprised the baseball world in 1987 by becoming world champions.

But Kirby Puckett was not expected to be a superstar. And while he had very fine seasons his first two years in the league, he continued to work, and the improvements in his game can be easily seen by some very revealing statistics.

In 1984 rookie Puckett came to bat 557 times for the Twins and failed to hit a home run. The next year Kirby had 691 official at-bats and hit just four homers. That's four home runs in nearly 700 trips to the plate. Then in 1986 Puckett came up another 680 times. Only now he connected for 31 homers. Yes, 31 homers! An increase like that is incredible, almost impossible.

But Puckett proved it wasn't a fluke, coming back in 1987 to bang out another 28 round-trippers. And unlike other players who suddenly hit more home runs, his batting average didn't drop. On the contrary, it rose, from .288 in 1985 to .328 in '86 and .332 in 1987. No wonder Kirby Puckett is considered one of baseball's hot new stars.

It all began for Kirby in Chicago, Illinois, where he was born on March 14, 1961. Life in an inner-city housing development on the south side of the city wasn't easy for the Puckett family. Kirby, one of nine children, spent his first 12 years living in a crowded 14th-floor apartment in an area where crime and drug addiction were rampant.

But it was a funny thing about Kirby, the youngest of the Puckett children. He always enjoyed baseball more than anything else.

"Street gangs and all that kind of stuff never meant anything to me," he said. "It just wasn't important. All I wanted to do was get home from school, do my homework, then look for a ball-game. If there wasn't anyone around, I'd just throw a ball up against a wall. Sometimes I just rolled up socks in my room and practiced that way. I loved baseball so much even then that I was always trying to think of ways to keep playing."

His mother, Catherine, remembers times when the older boys would hit Kirby's baseball so far that it would go over the nearby expressway and he was unable to get it back. She said there were times when he'd cry because his only baseball had been lost. But she also said the family did well under harsh conditions.

"Just because you live in a tough area doesn't mean you have to be like everyone else," she said. "What I mean is that people survived. We survived."

By the time Kirby reached Calumet High, he was a fine player and mainly a third baseman. He knew that third basemen were usually expected to hit with power, and at that time he didn't. He was a singles hitter who used his great speed to advantage. But he wanted more and, while still in high school, decided to change things.

"I knew I wasn't going to be tall," he explained, "so I decided the next best thing was to be strong."

That's when he began pumping iron—working with weights. While this greatly increased his strength, it didn't get him any offers when he graduated high school. He wasn't drafted and no college teams showed any interest. So he went to work, still dreaming of the only thing he loved— baseball.

In the summer of 1980, Kirby went to a Kansas City Royals tryout camp and was noticed by Dewey Kalmer, the coach at Bradley University. Kalmer offered him a scholarship, and the following spring Kirby was playing for Bradley. He was still raw, a wild swinger at the plate, and an erratic third baseman. But Dewey Kalmer saw his potential and his speed, and moved him to center field. That summer he began to blossom.

He was the second leading hitter in the Illinois Collegiate League with a .390 average for Quincy in 1981. But that fall tragedy struck. Kirby's father died, and to be closer to his mother, he enrolled at Triton Community College in River Grove, Illinois. All he did at Triton in 1982 was bat .472 with 16 home runs and 42 stolen bases. He was a terror in the outfield, his strong arm a threat to gun down any runner. He led Triton to the national junior college finals and was named Region IV Junior College Player of the Year.

With that kind of record it was no real surprise when he was the third player chosen in the 1982 draft, and shortly afterward he signed with Minnesota. His long-standing dream was becoming a reality.

At Elizabethtown in the Appalachian League, he batted .382 in 65 games and led the league in a number of offensive and defensive categories. He was an all-star and the Player of the Year. The only surprise was that in 275 at-bats, he hit just three home runs.

In 1983 he was at Visalia in the California League, where he was again Player of the Year, as well as Rookie of the Year and Best Batting Prospect. He hit .314 and swiped 48 bases. But once again the power was missing. He had 97 RBIs, but only nine homers in 548 at-bats. Yet he was promoted to Toledo, the Twins' top farm club, at the outset of the 1984 season.

He didn't stay there long. After playing just 21 games for Toledo at the beginning of the 1984 season, and despite just a .263 batting average and one home run, he was brought up to the Twins. On May 8, 1984, Kirby made his major league debut as the Twins center fielder. Playing against the California Angels, he became only the ninth player in the history of the game to get four hits in his first big-league game. And he's been the Twins' center fielder ever since.

Playing in 128 games in '84, Puckett batted .296 in 557 at-bats but failed to hit a single homer. But he was a valuable asset to his team nevertheless. He played a brilliant center field for a rookie, especially in the enclosed Metrodome, a notori-

In addition to being one of baseball's best hitters, Kirby Puckett is also an outstanding centerfielder. He plays center at Minnesota's Metrodome better than anyone and is shown here robbing an opposing hitter of a home run. *(Courtesy Minnesota Twins)*

ously tough field. He led the American League with 16 outfield assists and was also named to the all-rookie team.

In 1985 he really began to blossom. Playing in 161 games, Kirby led the majors in at-bats (691), outfield putouts (465), and total chances (492). He also finished in a tie with Boston's Dwight Evans when league managers voted for the outfielder with the best throwing arm. His batting average was a solid .288, he had 199 hits and drove home 74 runs. The only thing still missing was home-run power. With all those at-bats, Kirby managed just four round-trippers.

Maybe it was time to do something about it. After all, Kirby was a rock-solid 5′ 8″, 210 pounds, and very strong. His Twins coaches believed he should be able to hit the ball a lot farther and more often. Twins hitting coach Tony Oliva, himself a former American League batting champion, decided to work with the powerful young center fielder. He felt that Kirby was going to the opposite field too much and didn't know how to handle pitches that were coming in on him, the kind of pitches a strong hitter can put in the seats.

Oliva set out to teach Kirby how to pull the ball. He moved him closer to the plate and worked on keeping more weight on his back foot. He also took advantage of Puckett's strength and compact swing, teaching him to turn hard on inside pitches while still waiting long enough to get everything into it.

"Before I worked with Tony I was too anxious," Kirby said. "I didn't want pitchers to throw the ball past me, and I ended up lunging and hitting a lot of weak grounders."

Throughout spring training they worked, and Kirby began gaining confidence, getting the feeling that he could hit more home runs. Just getting him into double figures would have made the experiment a success. But no one, not even Kirby Puckett, could have predicted what would happen in 1986.

Kirby began the year like a house on fire. He was doing everything he had done before, only a little better. And at last he had added the one missing dimension to his game. He was hitting home runs. Oh, was he hitting home runs.

He hit his first homer early in the season. Not too many heads turned then. After all, everyone hits one once in a while. But on April 16 he went on a streak that had the entire baseball world talking. He was not only getting hits, but hitting home runs as well.

In a three-game series with the Angels, he homered in each of the first two games, and in the third had four hits in four trips. Against the Yankees in New York, he belted a 440-foot round-tripper to left center—an area hitters call Death Valley. In Detroit he took a Jack Morris pitch into the left-field seats despite a strong, 18-mile-per-hour wind blowing in.

He was named player of the month for April and, at the outset of May, walloped a Walt Terrell fastball deep into the seats. It was his 11th homer of the year, tops in the majors, and the 16th straight game in which he had hit safely. He was hitting .376 and leading the majors in runs, hits, extra-base hits, and slugging percentage.

"I thought I'd hit two or three homers a month this year," he said, "so this is like a dream. And last year you couldn't pay me to pull the ball. I just couldn't do it."

So Puckett had become a force to be reckoned with. He was always extremely likable and popular with both teammates and opponents. And now there was newfound respect for him as a player.

"What you have now is the complete ball-player," said Los Angeles Dodgers manager Tom Lasorda. "He's got speed, has a great arm, is outstanding defensively, hits for average and now with power. Plus he's a great human being."

That last statement was echoed by many. No one had a bad word to say about Kirby Puckett. He was liked by friend and foe on the field, and everybody off the field. His enthusiasm for the game was almost unusual in a businesslike era.

"I just love the game," Kirby said. "This is all fun for me, just like it was when I was a kid. I didn't play ball to get out of the ghetto. I played because I loved it. What more could I ask than to be in the big leagues?"

Others sensed it too. Mariners manager Dick Williams, one of baseball's tough guys, said this about Kirby.

"I just love watching him play. You can sense his enjoyment of the game. It just oozes from him out there. I'll tell you what, baseball could use a lot more Kirby Pucketts."

Teammate Al Newman put it this way. "He's always smiling. And no matter what happens, I've never heard him booed. I used to wonder how a guy built like him could hit and throw. Now I think he's the eighth wonder of the world."

When the 1986 season ended, Kirby Puckett was up with the league leaders in most offensive and defensive categories. He finished with a .328 batting average in 161 games. He also had 223 hits, 119 runs scored, 37 doubles, six triples, 31 homers, 96 runs batted in, and 20 stolen bases. He was on most of the all-star teams, and also won a Gold Glove as one of the league's three best outfielders. It was quite a year.

The only damper was the Twins being far off the pace in the American League West. It was hard to figure, for the club had some fine young ballplayers, including a quartet of sluggers who could hit with any group in the league. Joining Kirby in the power department were first baseman Kent

Hrbek, third sacker Gary Gaetti, and outfielder Tom Brunansky.

There were also some fine pitchers such as Frank Viola and veteran Bert Blyleven. But the club had been through a number of managers and seemed to disappoint every year. Then there were two important changes going into 1987. Tom Kelly was called in for his first full year as manager, and the club had acquired a bona fide bullpen stopper in Jeff Reardon.

In the early going, no team could seem to break open the A.L. West race. California, Kansas City, Oakland, the Twins, Texas, and even Seattle seemed to have a chance at one point. By midseason only the top four teams were still in it.

The Twins were playing brilliantly at home, indoors at the Metrodome, but they struggled on the road. In fact, for much of the year they had the best home record in all of baseball, and that's what kept them in the race.

As for Kirby Puckett, he was having still another brilliant season, showing the kind of consistency that all the great ones have. And he was still hitting home runs. He clobbered another at Yankee Stadium that fittingly bounced off the Babe Ruth monument in deep left center, a blast that teammate Tom Brunansky marveled at.

"I've hit a few big home runs," Brunansky said, "but never one like that."

The Twins continued battling for the division

lead. At one point they had a five-game lead, but shortly after the all-star break they went into a slump and fell out of first. Not coincidentally, Kirby Puckett also went into a slump, his average down to .315, and he wasn't hitting home runs. Then, in early September, the team traveled to Milwaukee to face the Brewers and Puckett exploded.

In the Saturday game, Kirby went four for five as the Twins routed the Brewers, 12–3. Then came the Sunday game. It was another slugfest, with Minnesota coming out on top, 10–6. But you could have easily called this one the Kirby Puckett Show.

All Kirby did was get six straight hits, including two homers and four RBIs. That gave him a record-tying 10 hits in two games. In addition, on Sunday, he made a leaping catch at the wall to rob the Brewers' Robin Yount of a grand slam home run. It was an amazing, superstar performance.

"It was just like old times," said Twins third baseman Gary Gaetti. "It showed again just how important Kirby Puckett is to us. He can carry a club. He really can."

Milwaukee's Paul Molitor, one of the better hitters in the league, concurred. "That's probably the most impressive one-day offensive performance I've seen in my 10 years in the big leagues," he said. "To hit six balls on the button like that is incredible."

Kirby, as usual, downplayed his achievement. "Sure, it's a day I'll never forget," he admitted, "but there's nothing more I can do about it now. It's all over and there's another game on Tuesday. I was just happy to contribute. The most important thing is that it was a win."

It was Puckett's hot streak that keyed a Twins surge that took them back to the top of the division. And when the season ended they were American League West champs with an 85–77 record. It was the poorest mark of any of the four division winners, but their 56–25 home mark was the best in baseball. On the road they were a poor 29–52. Still, they won the A.L. West crown.

Kirby, of course, had played an integral role in the victory. He batted a career high .332, with 28 homers and 99 RBIs. He also had a league-leading 207 hits. With a number of his teammates also having fine seasons, and Reardon giving them a stopper in the pen, the club was in the playoffs with a chance to go to the World Series.

In the A.L. playoffs, Minnesota would be facing the Detroit Tigers, a team with 98 victories and the best overall record in baseball. Even though the Twins were decided underdogs, a number of baseball people were calling for an upset.

It didn't take long to see that the Twins' big bats were getting loosened up for postseason play. In the first game against Detroit, Gaetti homered in each of his first two at-bats. That set the theme, and the Twins won it at home, 8–5.

"Gary showed we were capable of doing some damage," Manager Kelly said. "I think that was the key to getting us going on the right foot."

Something was going right. The Twins took the second game, 6–3, beating Tigers ace Jack Morris. Now they were in the driver's seat as the playoff series moved to Detroit. The Tigers managed to win the third, 7–6, and hoped that would get them back in it. But when the Twins took game four, 5–3, they had a commanding 3–1 lead.

In game five it was Bert Blyleven against Doyle Alexander, and the Twins wasted no time jumping to the lead. They knocked out Alexander with a four-run second. Brunansky drove in the first two runs with a double, Dan Gladden the third with a single, and Kirby got the fourth home with a base hit.

The Tigers closed in with three in the fourth, but the Twins got single runs in the seventh and eighth, then wrapped it up with three in the ninth for a 9–5 victory. They were American League champs and headed to the World Series.

There, the Twins met the St. Louis Cardinals, a team that had held off the defending champ New York Mets in an exciting National League East race. The Redbirds then beat the San Francisco Giants in seven hard-fought games. But the Cards were also coming into the series badly hurt. Their one renowned power hitter, Jack Clark, was out with a bad ankle. And their switch-hitting third baseman Terry Pendleton had a pulled rib-cage muscle that would only allow him to hit left-handed. He could only be used as a designated hitter or pinch hitter.

The series opened in Minnesota, and the noise in the Metrodome was deafening. Dan Gladden belted a grand slam home run to key a seven-run fourth inning, and the Twins coasted behind Frank Viola to take the opener, 10–1. Game two also featured a big fourth inning. This time Minnesota scored six times to win for Blyleven, 8–4. They had a 2–0 lead as the two clubs traveled to St. Louis for game three.

True to their season-long script, the Twins couldn't win on the road. The Cards took all three games, by scores of 3–1, 7–2, and 4–2, giving them a 3–2 lead and making the Twins' task a tough one. But the Twins knew they would be going home to the Metrodome once more. They also knew that there had never been a World Series in which the home team had won every game, so they had a tough order to fill.

Kirby had been having a very quiet series at the plate. As usual, he didn't let it get to him, and he kept taking his cuts and playing outstanding ball in center field. Finally, in the sixth game he began getting his stroke, slapping out three hits. And back in the Metrodome in front of their screaming fans, the Twins erupted again.

This time Kent Hrbek was the big hero, slamming a dramatic, bases-loaded homer off Ken Daley to key a series-tying 11–5 victory. The Cards had gambled, using their ace, John Tudor, in game six on three days' rest. The gamble backfired. Now it was time for the seventh and deciding game. Minnesota's ace Frank Viola was up against Cardinal rookie Joe McGrane.

The Cards drew first blood in the second, scoring a pair of runs on singles by Tony Peña and Steve Lake. Had the Redbirds finally solved the Metrodome riddle? Apparently not. In their half of the inning, Minnesota got one back as Steve Lombardozzi singled home the run. Then, in the fifth, the Twins tied the game on a single by shortstop Greg Gagne and a clutch double by Kirby Puckett. It might have been his biggest hit of the year, since it drew the Twins even. In the sixth Minnesota took the lead when Gagne drove home a run on an infield out.

Meanwhile, Frank Viola had settled down and was coasting. In the eighth a Gladden double scored Tim Laudner, and the Twins had a 4–2 lead. With the fans screaming on every pitch, Jeff Reardon came on and retired the Cards in the ninth. The Twins were world champs!

Some 200,000 Twins fans toasted the world champs in a huge parade a few days later. Frank

Viola was the MVP in a strange series that saw the Twins hit .329 in the Dome and just .184 in Busch Stadium. But they had defied the odds and won it, and that was the important thing.

As for Kirby Puckett, he was overjoyed, just like everyone else. It was the high spot of a career that was just four years old, yet had already seen him rise to become one of the acknowledged all-around superstars of the game. Married now, and a resident of Minneapolis, Kirby couldn't be happier.

"There's no prejudice in Minneapolis at all," he has said. "It's the kind of place you want your kids to grow up in. Even if I get traded someday, I'll keep a house in Minnesota."

There is little likelihood of that happening. The Twins are not about to part with a player like Kirby. After all, how many of today's athletes would say this:

"When I'm done with baseball, I'll call a press conference, thank everyone, and leave with dignity. Like a professional. I won't hang on for the money."

That's Kirby Puckett, a unique athlete and a unique man. And everyone knows it. As his manager, Tom Kelly, has said:

"Something about the guy just makes you feel good."

Roger Clemens

One of the most awesome sights in baseball is the power pitcher, the fastballer, blowing smoke past frustrated hitters. To watch guys like Bob Gibson, Sandy Koufax, and Nolan Ryan getting stronger in the late innings and challenging one hitter after another is something a fan won't soon forget.

There aren't a whole lot of pure power pitchers, maybe just one or two in each generation. Nolan Ryan still qualifies. In 1987, past the age of 40, the Houston fireballer again led the major leagues in strikeouts with 270. But who else? Dwight Gooden of the Mets? His talent is immense. Yet in the past two seasons he has dominated less than he did in his brilliant Cy Young year of 1985.

The American League? Just one name comes to mind: Roger Clemens of the Boston Red Sox.

Roger Clemens *(Courtesy Boston Red Sox)*

Clemens took the baseball world by storm in 1986, winning his first 14 decisions en route to an incredible 24–4 season, a season in which he set a new record by striking out 20 batters in a single game. That's power. He was so good, in fact, that he also captured both the Cy Young and Most Valuable Player awards.

For an encore in 1987, Clemens overcame a lengthy contract squabble and holdout to post a 20–9 record. And in the final months of the season he was again the most dominating pitcher in baseball, a power pitcher with the ability to blow an entire team away.

It happened to the hard-hitting Milwaukee Brewers in the final game of the 1987 season. Roger Clemens was on the mound gunning for his 20th win, and he wasn't to be denied. He throttled the Brewers on just two hits, facing just 29 batters, two over the minimum. He struck out 12, walked none. And he did it on just three days' rest and after a game in which he had thrown 160 pitches. That's power.

"He was on a mission," said Paul Molitor, who earlier in the year had compiled a 41-game hitting streak. "He just overmatched us. It was no contest."

That's a power pitcher. He can overmatch even the best of hitters when he's got his best stuff. And Roger Clemens certainly qualifies. He was just 23 years old when he had his banner 24–4 season. He was coming off two consecutive seasons in which arm problems short-circuited him. These finally led to shoulder surgery, which made him a questionable commodity. He overcame his problems through hard work, something that has been his trademark ever since he was a youngster.

Roger William Clemens was born on August 4, 1962, in Dayton, Ohio. He was one of six children and Roger, along with the rest of the family, suffered a severe blow when their father died. Roger was just nine at the time, and looked to his brother Randy for guidance.

"Randy was 10 years older than me," Roger said. "He became my father image and I tried to do everything he did. I really think that helped me."

Because Randy was into sports, Roger followed, and he excelled from the first. By the time Roger reached high school, the family had moved to Houston, Texas. That's where he first began making a name as an athlete.

"Wherever Roger went," said brother Randy, "championships seemed to follow."

He started by leading Houston's Spring Woods High School to the Texas schoolboy title. As a pitcher–first baseman he was able to contribute on an everyday basis. He played the same dual role for his American Legion team, and sure enough, they won the state championship in 1979. Besides baseball, he was a defensive end on his high school football team and played center in basketball.

His coach at Spring Woods, Charlie Maiorana, said that Roger was different even then, that his work habits were always a cut above those of the other good players on the team.

"We had pretty vigorous workouts then," Maiorana said, "with a lot of running. Yet Roger would always jog home from practice, carrying a heavy duffel bag with all his stuff in it. And after he made it to the majors, he would come out to our ballpark to work out before spring training. And he still jogged, never walked or rode."

Following his high school graduation, Roger spent two years at San Jacinto Junior College in Houston, where he was named an all-American. Then in June of 1981, he learned that he was the 12th draft pick of the New York Mets, who also drafted a young pitcher named Dwight Gooden that year. But Roger felt he wasn't yet ready for pro ball and declined to sign. Instead he enrolled at the University of Texas.

Once again he excelled, becoming an all-American twice more. His two-year record at Texas was 25–7 with 241 strikeouts. And his second year he pitched the Longhorns to the College World Series, winning the title game against Alabama, 4–3.

This time the Red Sox drafted him as number one. He wasn't quite 21 years old when he began his professional career with Winter Haven. He went 3–1 in four starts with a 1.24 earned run average and was promptly promoted to New Britain, where he went 4–1 with a 1.38 ERA. His combined strikeout total was 95 in just 81 innings. The Red Sox knew they had something special.

At 6' 4", 215 pounds, Roger possesses a fastball that travels in excess of 95 miles per hour. He's an imposing sight out on the mound, and when 1984 rolled around, the Sox started him off at Pawtucket, their top farm team. They then called him up to the majors on May 11, at the age of 21.

Once in the rotation, Roger did well. By August he had found his stride. He won four straight games, and was named American League pitcher of the month. That brought his season's record to 9–4. But on August 31, his year ended suddenly when he suffered an injury to his right forearm.

In 1985 he was back and hoping to do better. But in late May he began experiencing shoulder problems. He finally had to go on the disabled list, and on August 30 underwent arthroscopic shoulder surgery. It wasn't considered a serious problem, but as Roger said, "It was very scary."

Roger was 7–5 when his season ended this time, and now there had to be some question about the future. There always is when a pitcher has any kind of arm or shoulder operation. You never know what the result will be, especially for a power pitcher like Clemens, who relies so much on his great velocity. So he was looked upon as "iffy" for 1986.

But the big guy never rested. He began working with weights immediately after the surgery, determined to come to camp in the best possible shape. Even after a hard workout at the ballpark he always ran an extra two miles.

"Then I'd collapse in bed," he explained. "But the extra running is better than going out for a beer. Beer isn't going to make me a better pitcher."

It was this kind of attitude that helped Roger bounce back and be more than ready when 1986 began. But while he was ready to play baseball, baseball wasn't quite ready for Roger Clemens. Because he was coming off shoulder surgery and really in his first full year, he took the baseball world by surprise, and by storm. He wasn't the friendliest guy to the media in the spring, so after a while, there wasn't much communication. But Roger had a reason for his diffidence.

"After my surgery, I decided I was going to put everything I had into coming back," he said. "I didn't talk much in spring training because I had a job to do and I had to concentrate 100 percent on that job."

The Red Sox had a sound team in 1986, with such stars as Wade Boggs, Dwight Evans, Jim Rice, Rich Gedman, Bill Buckner, and Marty Barrett, and pitchers Bruce Hurst, Dennis "Oil Can"

Boyd, and Bob Stanley. But the club lacked an ace, a stopper, and no one really picked them to win the American League East. The Bosox hadn't won since 1975, and they had a reputation as a team that always found a way to fade.

Roger was impressive in his first three outings, winning them all and showing everyone that he was completely recovered from the surgery. His fastball was clocked in the mid-90s, and his sharp curve kept hitters off balance. Despite this, no one was prepared for what was about to happen on the night of April 29 as Clemens took the mound to face the Seattle Mariners.

Roger had his good stuff that night. In fact, it was great stuff. His fastball was clocked at 97 miles per hour, and his curve was catching the corners of the plate. And the Mariners couldn't hit him. Batter after batter was going down on strikes as the big right-hander kept firing away. When the smoke cleared, Clemens and the Red Sox had a 3–1 victory. What's more, the big guy had struck out 20 Mariners to set a new major league record.

Now the Sox could hide Clemens no longer. Roger had broken a record shared by Nolan Ryan, Steve Carlton, and Tom Seaver, all future Hall of Famers. Even his manager, John McNamara, who had seen a lot of the great ones, couldn't contain his enthusiasm.

"I've never seen a pitching performance as awesome as that," McNamara said. "And I don't think you'll ever see one again in the history of baseball."

Roger Clemens disagreed, and for the first time expressed the tremendous confidence he had in himself—and also his tremendous devotion to the game of baseball.

"If anyone has a chance to do it again, it's me," he said. "And if that sounds cocky, so be it. I've got to be cocky when I'm on the mound. After all, that's half my life out there. And I did a lot of work to get where I am. I've always worked hard."

Teammate Dwight Evans agreed. Evans had been with the Red Sox since the early 1970s, and was quite impressed with the big young pitcher.

"Hang around with Roger for a week and you'll see he's always working, always doing something," Evans said, "whether it's running, lifting weights, or just studying the hitters."

Whatever Roger was doing, he was doing it right. He continued to win as the Red Sox jumped atop the division. And when his winning streak hit double figures, even more people began noticing. After he ran his record to 11–0 it was noted that he had the best opening win streak since the Yanks' Ron Guidry went 13–0 in 1978. And more and more fans began asking the same question. When is Roger Clemens going to lose a game?

When he won his 14th straight he was just one game short of the league record. Then came a game against the Toronto Blue Jays at Fenway Park on July 2. Clemens took a 2–1 lead into the eighth inning, but the Blue Jays scored three runs to pull the game out, 4–2. The streak was over, but Roger Clemens was not about to fold.

He started the All-Star Game for the American League with a 15–2 record, pitched three perfect innings, and became the winning pitcher and all-star MVP. Then he took up where he left off, pitching the Red Sox to an American League pennant.

His dominance continued in the second half. He was a true stopper—14 of his victories came following a Bosox loss. He won his final seven decisions to finish the season with an incredible 24–4 mark. Though he pitched only one shutout, his earned run average was a fine 2.48 and he fanned 238 hitters in 254 innings. Opposing batters could only compile a .195 average off his serves during the year. He was without a doubt *the* major league pitcher of 1986.

In the playoffs that year, the Sox had to face the California Angels. With Roger Clemens on the mound, game one seemed a lock. But Roger had a rare off day and the Angels won it behind Mike Witt, 8–1. When he pitched again in the fourth game he took a 3–0 lead into the ninth. But the Angels rallied and Roger left still leading, 3–1, with one out and two on. The relievers couldn't hold it and he wound up with a no-decision as

California won in the 11th, to take a 3–1 lead in the playoffs.

But the Bosox battled back to tie it. They were just one strike away from elimination when they rallied to take game five. They won the sixth, 10–4, then sent Roger back to the mound for the seventh and deciding game.

Despite being weakened by the flu, Roger went right at the Angels' hitters. He threw seven innings of one-run ball and the Sox won the pennant-clinching game, 8–1. Then they moved on to the World Series against the New York Mets.

Though it was an exciting series, one that the Sox came within a solitary strike of winning, Roger wasn't really a deciding factor. Maybe it was just too much pitching in his first full year in the majors. He went just four and a third innings in game two, and while the Sox won it, 9–3, he failed to get a decision. In the sixth game, with a chance to wrap it up, he was sharper. In fact, he didn't give up a hit until the fifth.

He gave up just two runs, one earned, in seven innings, and left with a 3–2 lead. But once again the Sox relievers could not hold it, and the Mets tied the series, then won it in a seventh game. Roger had a 3.18 ERA in his two series games, and fanned 11 in 11⅓ innings. Yet he wasn't quite as dominant as he had been all season long.

He had an incredible year, one that ended with him winning that rare double, the Cy Young

A power pitcher all the way, Roger Clemens can be simply overpowering. He was the American League's Cy Young Award winner in both 1986 and 1987. *(Courtesy Boston Red Sox)*

Award as the league's best pitcher as well as the American League Most Valuable Player Award. Now the question was, what could he do for an encore?

"I don't care who you are," Roger said, "every year you've got to come in and prove yourself again. I'll start next year at 0–0, just like everyone else. I'm a nobody and I'll have to prove myself just like anybody else."

So he continued to work hard. But there was a problem, which became even clearer as spring training for 1987 approached. Roger and the Red Sox couldn't agree on a new contract, and at the beginning of training camp, he was missing, a holdout.

"I had to do what was best for me," he said. "I just wanted to be recognized for what I did on the field because I put a lot of hard work into it. But I didn't want what I did to affect the fans."

So while the rest of the Sox honed their skills at spring training, Roger Clemens, considered by many the best pitcher in baseball, was back home playing pitch and catch with high school players.

After a 29-day holdout, the contract dispute was solved, but Roger was still way behind everyone when the season began. And the rust showed. He obviously wasn't the same pitcher. Though he split his first four decisions, Roger remained optimistic.

"I don't feel the layoff hurt me," he said. "And I

still don't see a lot of problems in trying to accomplish what I've always done. That's to be consistent and win." Roger's slow start was compounded by other Sox problems. Catcher Gedman was another holdout and couldn't return until May. Oil Can Boyd was having arm problems and was out of the rotation. Jim Rice was not having a good year and the team just wasn't winning.

For Roger, the struggle to regain his form continued. On June 12 he was pasted by the Detroit Tigers, 11–4, dropping his record to 4–6 and raising his earned run average to 3.51.

"That hasn't really been me out there," Roger said. "I think I've just been trying to do too much."

Maybe he was right. Or perhaps he needed those games to really get sharp after his long holdout. But soon after losing to the Tigers, he began coming on, pitching more like the 1986 version. By the all-star break he was back over .500. And he continued to pitch well.

Despite a bout with the flu, he shut out the California Angels, 3–0, getting the whitewash even though he failed to fan a single batter. But in his next outing against Seattle, he was once again his old, overpowering self, fanning 14 Mariners en route to an 11–1 triumph that raised his record to 10–7 for the year.

"He was on the corners all day long," said Red Sox shortstop Spike Owen. "It was a classic performance with a fastball and breaking ball."

And there was more to come. In the second half of 1987, Roger Clemens was again every bit the pitcher he had been in '86, maybe even better. And this time he was doing it with a team that was out of the race and playing below .500 ball. This made his pitching even more impressive.

When he began to feel he had a shot at winning 20 games once again, he really turned it on for a spectacular finish, culminating with his awesome, final-day victory over Milwaukee, which gave him a 20–9 log for the year. Had he not held out, he might have easily duplicated his 1986 record. And still, in some ways, he surpassed it.

For instance, in 1987 he led the majors with 18 complete games, compared with 10 in '86. He also led all major league hurlers with seven shutouts. He had only thrown one in all of 1986. He was second in innings pitched, with 281, and in strikeouts with 256. In his last 16 starts he was 12–2 with a 2.03 ERA, and after the beating in Detroit that had left him at 4–6, he went 16–3 for the balance of the year. All this with a club that finished with a 78–84 record. To top it off, he won a second straight Cy Young prize.

Always slightly the rebel, very much his own man, and a devoted family man as well, Roger

Clemens could well be baseball's next superstar pitcher. He's well on the way with two straight super seasons and he's still just 25 years old.

But nothing has been given to him. Hard work has always been his trademark and there's no reason to think he'll change. For Roger Clemens knows that nobody gives you anything. You've got to earn it. That's precisely what he's done. Just ask any hitter in the American League.

Darryl Strawberry

Some years ago there was a hotshot basketball player coming out of college and entering the National Basketball Association. A major sports magazine did a profile piece on him with the title "The Burden of Great Expectations." That title, in a sense, describes the career of Darryl Strawberry in the major leagues.

Strawberry is the star right fielder of the New York Mets, a player who came into the game expected to be one of the greatest ever. That's an unfair burden for any athlete to bear. And because the Straw Man, as he is sometimes called, has yet to reach the lofty heights predicted for him, his stay in the media fishbowl of New York hasn't always been easy.

Darryl Strawberry (*Courtesy National Baseball Library, Cooperstown, New York*)

Standing 6' 6" tall and weighing a rock-solid 195 pounds, Darryl has the ability to hit the ball a country mile. And, indeed, he has belted some mammoth home runs. But, because he still hasn't responded with the super season everyone has predicted, Strawberry still suffers the curse of unfulfilled potential.

"It's the price you have to pay in New York," Darryl has said. "You're only human. You can't do everything right. But you can't hide from it in New York. You've got to face it. But sometimes I think people are asking too much."

It really began for Darryl Strawberry long before he came to New York. While Darryl was starring at Crenshaw High in Los Angeles, his coach, Brooks Hurst, was the first to say it.

"You could be a black Ted Williams," he told Darryl.

The label stuck. Williams, of course, was one of the greatest hitters ever, belting 521 home runs and batting .344 during a long career twice interrupted by military service. He was also the last major leaguer to hit over .400 in a season, batting .406 in 1941.

Like Williams, young Strawberry is long and angular, and a left-handed hitter with a powerful stroke. And also as with Williams, great expectations followed Darryl to the major leagues. Former Mets manager George Bamberger, when talking about Darryl, said this:

"Fifteen years from now this kid will turn out to be one of the greatest ever to play the game."

Another former Mets skipper, Frank Howard, was no less enthusiastic when talking about young Strawberry.

"If we miss on this young man," Howard said, "we all better look for a career change. He can go as far in this game as any man today."

And so it continued. Since joining the Mets early in the 1983 season, Darryl Strawberry has been under a microscope. Today, he is considered a superstar, and is paid a superstar's salary. In fact, the 1987 season was possibly his best ever. He hit a career-high 39 home runs, drove in 104 runs, and had a .284 batting average. But with that, there was controversy, and there were questions about Darryl's ability to fulfill that enormous potential. Mets fans must often wonder, will it ever end?

It began in Los Angeles, where Darryl grew up the third of five children born to Henry and Ruby Strawberry. The Strawberrys separated when Darryl was 13, and after that he was raised mainly by his mother.

Like many top athletes, sports dominated Darryl's life from the time he was a young boy. He played in the playgrounds and parks of Los Angeles every chance he had. A neighbor of the Strawberrys, John Moseley, who was an assistant baseball coach at Compton College, often took the Strawberry boys to the park and drilled them in the fundamentals of the game.

"Baseball was all Darryl ever talked about," Moseley recalled. "He was the kind of guy who didn't even mess around with girls. He was just a baseball fanatic."

Moseley also gave the boys fatherly advice from time to time, telling them to study in school and avoid getting in trouble on the streets.

"I'd say to them, how are you going to play ball with a broken hand? So don't go punching anyone around."

Darryl himself gives John Moseley credit for teaching him everything he knows about the game, or at least being the first to teach him. He also admits that when he first arrived at Crenshaw High he was unhappy and often moody.

"I carried around a bad attitude," he said. "I guess I figured I didn't have to listen to anyone or do anything."

His attitude and lack of hustle eventually got him suspended from the team, and it wasn't until he asked to be reinstated and got a second chance that he began to straighten out his act.

"Getting thrown off the team was the best thing that happened to me back then," he says now.

Finally, in his junior and senior years he became an outstanding player, in both baseball and basketball, and as a senior he batted .400 with five homers and 18 RBIs. He was one of the top-rated high school players in the country, a player who hated to lose a game.

In June of 1980, he became the number-one draft choice of the Mets, the first player taken in the free agent draft that year. And with everyone predicting greatness for him, he headed for Kingsport, Tennessee, to play in the Rookie League.

Suffering from a case of homesickness, Strawberry did poorly. Some Mets officials wondered if they had made a mistake. He could only muster a .268 average with five homers and 20 RBIs. Yet in 1981 he was at Lynchburg, and finally began to blossom. He finished with 13 homers and 78 RBIs, but not without struggling in the early going. One of his teammates there, catcher Lloyd McClendon, thought part of the problem was the pressure of being a top draft choice.

"He had a hard time handling it," McClendon said. "There were times when he went into a shell, and other times when he talked about going home. I tried to encourage him and to improve his work habits. He just wasn't getting himself ready to play the games."

A year later Darryl was at Jackson in the Texas League and playing like a different person—the one the Mets thought they had drafted out of Crenshaw High. He walloped 34 home runs, drove in 97, and became the league's Most Valuable Player.

Then, at the beginning of the 1983 season, there was more controversy surrounding him. This time it wasn't of his making. The Mets were a team in transition and many observers felt there should be an immediate spot on the team for Darryl Strawberry. He was just 21 years old, but people were already looking to him as the team's savior. Pressure once more.

Finally, despite an excellent spring, the Mets decided to send Darryl to their top farm club at Tidewater for more seasoning. But it didn't last long. The Mets got off to a terrible start and by the first week in May they recalled the Straw Man. The town erupted in anticipation. Darryl came to Shea Stadium in New York on May 6 for his first major league game. He faced Cincinnati's ace right-hander, Mario Soto.

It turned out to be a humbling experience. Soto fanned Strawberry three times and popped him up the fourth. He looked bad.

"I remember after the game thinking that I hadn't seen stuff like that in the minor leagues," Darryl commented.

That first game turned out to be a sign of things to come. The next two months were a nightmare. Darryl couldn't break out of a horrendous slump, and some of the same people who clamored for him to be brought up now demanded he be sent back down. But to the Mets' credit, they stuck with him.

"It was the toughest time of my life," Darryl said. "Being in the majors and playing in front of all those people was almost frightening to me. It even gave me the jitters when I'd hear my name announced. I wanted to hit home runs just to show people what I could do. But I began pressing, overswinging, trying to uppercut everything. And I think I was trying to save the ballclub."

By June 5 Strawberry was struggling with a .161 average and talk of his being a savior stopped. But he stayed in the lineup and gradually began snapping out of it. The home runs began to come, and each time a circuit shot leaped off Darryl's bat, there were visions of him leading the Mets to the promised land.

Over the final 54 games of the year he hit .313 with 14 homers and 34 RBIs and for the year finished with a .257 batting average, 26 homers, and 74 runs batted in. Despite the terrible start, he wound up being named National League Rookie of the Year.

It was quite a comeback, and one that augured well for 1984. He spent the winter taking batting practice near his mother's home in Los Angeles and returned as a 22-year-old claiming he was about to become a team leader.

"Leadership is just another challenge for me," he said. "I know I'm tired of hearing how bad this ballclub is."

In truth, the Mets were slowly rebuilding. They

had some solid veterans like Keith Hernandez and Rusty Staub, some good young players in Mookie Wilson and Hubie Brooks, and a 19-year-old pitcher who looked like he was going to be a great one. His name was Dwight Gooden. Ron Darling was still another young pitcher expected to be a winner.

Darryl put together a solid year in 1984, but to some it was a disappointment. Playing in 147 games, he hit just .251, six points below his rookie year. With 102 additional at-bats, he hit 26 home runs for the second year in succession, although his RBIs were up to 97.

In 1985, the Mets became a contender. The team made a major trade, acquiring veteran catcher Gary Carter from Montreal in return for Hubie Brooks and two other players. Carter was a leader, a power hitter who always drove in a lot of runs. He provided needed stability both in the lineup and behind the plate.

With the season started, something else became obvious. Twenty-year-old Dwight Gooden, in just his second season, was the best pitcher in baseball. The Doctor, as he was called, was en route to an incredible 24–4 year in which he would capture the attention of the entire baseball world. So Darryl Strawberry was no longer the center of attention.

But while the Mets looked much better in '85, Darryl started slowly. In the first 24 games of the year he was hitting just .215 with six homers and 12 ribbys. In the 25th game, he tried to make a diving catch in right field and tore ligaments in his right thumb. He sat out some 51 games.

When he returned, the Mets were chasing the St. Louis Cardinals in the National League East race. And suddenly Darryl Strawberry became an important part of that race. In the final 86 games of the season, the Straw Man had 23 homers and 67 RBIs. Though the Mets finished second, Strawberry compiled a fine season, hitting .277 in 111 games, with a career-high 29 home runs and with 79 RBIs. In a sense, it was beginning to look as if he was finally coming of age. He felt it, and so did some others.

"I think it's coming," Darryl said. "It's just a matter of time. I'm feeling more confident and relaxed. It's been three years now, and I feel I'm maturing. I think I'm ready to have the kind of year I'm capable of."

"Darryl," said pitcher Ed Lynch, "is just waiting to explode."

"When he stays in there and drives the ball," said batting coach Bill Robinson, "he has a chance to be as good as they come. This should be his year. The growing pains should be behind him."

In reality, 1986 was the Mets' year. They had built a well-balanced team, with a perfect combination of youngsters and veterans, and a pitch-

The Straw Man at the plate can end a game with one quick swing of his mighty bat. Many of his home runs are of the tape measure variety. *(Courtesy National Baseball Library, Cooperstown, New York)*

ing staff second to none. The starting rotation of Gooden, Darling, Bob Ojeda, Sid Fernandez, and Rick Aguilera was the best in baseball.

Hernandez, Carter, and Strawberry formed a great 1-2-3 punch in the heart of the lineup. The bullpen was strong with Jesse Orosco and Roger McDowell, and players such as Ray Knight, Mookie Wilson, Wally Backman, Rafael Santana, Tim Teufel, Lenny Dykstra, Kevin Mitchell, and Howard Johnson all contributed to the total team effort.

The Mets ran away with the National League East, winning 108 games in the process. Everything fell into place—it was no contest right from the start.

A number of Mets put together fine seasons. For most players, the stats compiled by Darryl Strawberry would have been most satisfying. He led the team with 27 homers and was second to Carter with 93 ribbys. But his batting average was just .259. And while he stole 28 bases, he missed some more time to injury and had just 475 at-bats.

Once again there were questions. New York is a tough town to play in, and the attention and hype from the press never lets up. After all, Darryl had been pretty much consistent since his rookie year, but he had not yet put up superstar numbers, at least the numbers expected of him. When, for instance, was he going to hit .300, or close to it?

And when would he have that 40-to-50-homer season, with maybe 120-to-130 RBIs?

But Darryl and his teammates had better things to worry about than the media—the playoffs and World Series.

The playoffs were against the Houston Astros, and it turned out to be an exciting and hard-fought series. Houston's ace pitcher, Mike Scott, a former Met, bested Gooden in game one, 1–0, striking out 14 Mets. Bob Ojeda got the Mets even in the second as Darryl drove in one run in a 5–1 victory.

Game three saw Darryl hit a clutch, three-run homer to tie the game in the sixth inning. But Houston regained the lead and it took a Lenny Dykstra two-run homer in the bottom of the ninth to win it, 6–5.

In game four the Mets were baffled by Scott again, 3–1, but they took game five, 2–1, behind Gooden and Jesse Orosco. The New Yorkers won this one in the 12th inning on a Gary Carter hit. They reached the 12th because Darryl had homered to tie the game in the fifth. Now, the Mets wanted to win it in game six, because they feared facing Mike Scott again in game seven.

Game six of the playoffs turned out to be one of the all-time great games of baseball history. Houston got three in the first off Bob Ojeda, and those runs held up until the top of the ninth, when miraculously the Mets rallied to tie it. The game went to extra innings, and both teams scored a run in the 14. Then, in the 16th, the Mets got three more, only to see Houston rally and almost tie it again. But Jesse Orosco hung in to get the save, as the Mets won it, 7–6, and were National League champs!

Darryl was just five for 22 in the series with Houston, but he led the club with two homers and five RBIs. Now he and his teammates got ready for the World Series against the Boston Red Sox. The Sox won the opener, 1–0, as Bruce Hurst bested Ron Darling. Then the Sox poured it on in the second game, winning 9–3 behind Roger Clemens. They had a 2–0 lead with the series headed to Boston. And Darryl had been hitless in both games.

In Boston things turned around. The Mets won game three, 7–1, behind Ojeda, then took the fourth, 6–2, with Ron Darling doing the pitching. Straw finally got some hits, but no ribbys. In game five, the Sox chased Gooden and Bruce Hurst won his second, 4–2, giving the Bosox a 3–2 lead as the series returned to Shea.

Game six was a miracle. It was knotted at three at the end of nine, but in the top of the 10th the Sox got a pair to go ahead, 5–3. The Mets had one last chance, and when their first two hitters went out, it looked over. One out away from losing the series, Gary Carter singled, and after that the team rallied. Mitchell singled, Knight singled to get a run in. A wild pitch got a second run home. And then Mookie Wilson hit a grounder to first that went through Bill Buckner's legs to allow Knight to scamper home with the winning run.

The next night, the Mets became world champs with an 8–5 come-from-behind victory. And in the bottom of the eighth, Darryl poled a long home run. He circled the bases slowly, savoring the moment, for he had not had a good series and had been ridden incessantly by the Boston fans. At least he had some measure of revenge.

Darryl had batted just .208 in the series with his only RBI coming on the eighth-inning homer in game seven. It was still another disappointment and he could only hope to atone in 1987.

That was the year the Mets had problems. It started in the spring when Dwight Gooden admitted he had used drugs and would miss the first month of the season in rehabilitation. Several trades and personnel changes also upset the chemistry of the team. Then an uncanny number of injuries to the pitching staff hurt them further. As a result, the team got off to a terrible start.

Oddly enough, Darryl got off to a fast start, belting a bunch of early-season homers and looking as if he was finally going to put together the super season everyone was waiting for. But there were some problems. In spring training he was fined $1,500 for missing two workouts. Then, in

Chicago in early June, he was fined for arriving late for batting practice.

When he sat out of a big game with the Cards in July, claiming he wasn't feeling well, the problems really started. Veteran Lee Mazzilli was the first to speak out.

"What Darryl did was let his manager down, let his coaches down, and most importantly, let his teammates down."

Darryl replied, "I'm sick. I had been feeling it for a few days. I didn't want to play and hurt the club."

But then second baseman Wally Backman added, "From the stuff I hear in the trainers' room, he should have been out there. Nobody in the world I know gets sick 25 times a year. There's only so much you can take."

That did it. Darryl threatened to do bodily harm to Backman and Mazzilli, and while he later came to terms with Mazzilli, the word was he stayed angry with Backman. He also began talking like someone who didn't feel he was appreciated.

"Where would this team be without me?" he asked. "So I miss a couple of games. When I'm gone from here, they'll wonder why I left."

Darryl wasn't the only one to come under criticism. When a team that's supposed to win loses, those things happen. Ron Darling was chided for having too many outside interests, and though Gooden was back and winning, there were some who still blamed his drug problem for part of the team's slow start.

Though the Mets made a late-season run at it, they fell short and were dethroned by the Cards. Yet with all his problems, Darryl Strawberry managed to put together his finest season. He had career highs in batting average (.284), homers (39), and RBIs (104). Once again, he seems on the brink of really busting out.

In a way, the Straw Man is at a crossroads. The tremendous ability and potential is still there. Strawberry will be just 26 years old in 1988. There are some questions about his desire. Does he want it badly enough? It would seem that he does. What player wouldn't want to be at the top of his profession?

But it hasn't been an easy road. Darryl Strawberry has been a Rookie of the Year and a world champion in his short career. And his numbers have been consistent, if not great. Still, there have been rumors that he'd welcome a trade to the Dodgers or another West Coast team. But it's difficult to see the Mets parting with his awesome talent.

The burden of great expectations. For Darryl Strawberry, it very well could be a burden he will always have to bear.

José Canseco

When you stand 6′ 3″ tall, weigh a muscular 230 pounds, and can hit a baseball a country mile, prospects for the future are bright. In fact, that's something of an understatement. With the money professional baseball players can make today, the future for someone fitting that description is fantastic.

But there are also pitfalls. A young ballplayer has to keep things in perspective. He must keep his priorities in order if he expects to become a complete ballplayer and have a long, successful career. In other words, he must work at it. Natural talent will take you just so far.

In this sense, the jury is still out on José Canseco, the 6′ 3″, 230-pound left fielder of the Oakland A's. José burst on the scene as a 21-year-

José Canseco (*Courtesy Oakland A's*)

old in 1986, and immediately began belting home runs like a Mickey Mantle, Dave Kingman, or Reggie Jackson. He hit long, high, skyrocketing drives into the far reaches of some of the biggest ballparks in the American League. By all-star break time of his rookie year, greatness was already being predicted of him. The question was, could he fulfill his awesome potential? Or might he become a one-dimensional ballplayer capable only of hitting an occasional mammoth home run?

One important thing in José's favor is he's not alone, for if he were, the glare of publicity might overwhelm him. On the contrary, José came up at a time when there was a whole group of young sluggers, especially in the American League. And he also appeared on the scene at a time when there was a controversy over the baseball itself, and whether it had been juiced up. For it seems that even little guys were hitting more home runs than ever before.

José Canseco, however, is not a little guy. He's a big strong kid who came out of nowhere to belt 33 homers and drive in 117 runs and earn himself the Rookie of the Year award for 1986. Another rookie, Wally Joyner of the California Angels, also felt he was good enough to win it, while a number of other young sluggers were also hanging up impressive numbers.

In a sense, the presence of other young sluggers might have helped take José out of the spotlight, but it also creates a competitive situation that could lead all the youngsters to push themselves to new heights.

Canseco's rise to stardom was rather meteoric in itself, but had other circumstances not been just right, he may never have played in the big leagues at all. You see, José Canseco was born on July 2, 1964, in Havana, Cuba, a country tangled in the web of Fidel Castro's communist dictatorship. And while Cuba had produced a number of outstanding major league players in the 1950s and into the 1960s, the Bay of Pigs confrontation between the United States and Cuba in 1961 and the Cuban Missile Crisis of 1962 all but closed Cuban immigration to the United States.

But somehow, José Canseco, Sr., managed to get his family out of Havana and to Miami, Florida, in 1965. With him were his wife, Barbara, and their nine-month-old twin boys, José, Jr., and Osvaldo, as well as their sister, Teresa. So it was on to a new life. Mr. Canseco went to work in Miami and raised his family there.

Thus the children learned to speak English before they spoke Spanish, and it still surprises people that José doesn't speak with a Spanish accent.

"I guess it's because people know I was born in Cuba," he said, "that they expect me to speak in broken English. But that's really funny, because I wasn't even a year old when we came here."

Mr. Canseco also admits that his children all

spoke English first, but he didn't want it to end there.

"I wanted all my children to be bilingual," he said, "to speak both English and Spanish. After all, it is our heritage. So José speaks Spanish as well, but he's not as fluent as I am."

When the family first came to Florida they first lived in the Opa-Locka section of Miami, but later moved to the southwest section of the city, where Mr. Canseco went to work for an oil company. And his twin boys prepared to enter Coral Park High School.

By that time the boys were tall, but still very thin. They were already fine baseball players, having grown up with the game as an all-year-round activity in the warm climate of Florida.

"I was about six foot one when I started high school," José remembered, "but I only weighed about 155 pounds. I think that might have held me back, because I didn't play varsity ball until my senior year. And when I graduated I think I weighed about 170."

In his senior year at Coral Park High, José began to blossom. He hit an even .400, and was named to the All-Greater Miami Athletic Conference first team, and he began attracting the attention of major league scouts.

One of the first to notice him was Camilo Pascual, a scout for the Oakland A's, and a Cuban-born former major leaguer who won 174 games during a fine pitching career. José and Osvaldo had played ball with Pascual's son, as well as with Danny Tartabull, the son of another former major leaguer, Cuban-born José Tartabull. Danny Tartabull would eventually enter the majors the same year as José, and also become one of the fine young sluggers in the game.

After his outstanding senior year at Coral Park, José waited for the major league draft. After all, he'd only really had one good season. But the potential was there and Camilo Pascual saw it. He persuaded the A's to draft José on the 15th round. Brother Osvaldo was originally drafted as a pitcher by the Yanks, then later converted to the outfield. He has since been traded to the A's organization, so there is a chance that the two brothers may yet be teammates in the big leagues.

But José was the more advanced of the two, and he began his professional career at Miami in the Florida State League. He played just nine games there before being moved up to Idaho Falls of the Pioneer League. There, in 28 games, he batted .263 with just two homers and seven RBIs in 57 at-bats. But he was barely 18 years old and still filling out physically.

He began the 1983 season at Madison, played 34 games there, and hit just .159 with three homers, then moved on to Medford of the Northwest League, another single-A team. At Medford he finally began showing signs of awakening at the plate. In 59 games he hit .269, including 11 homers and 40 RBIs. He also led the league by striking out 78 times.

Nevertheless, his talent was apparent to everyone. He was voted the Best Hitting Prospect and Hitter with the Best Power in a league poll, and was the all-star designated hitter. The A's were watching his development carefully now. His weight was up over 200 pounds and his big swing had power written all over it. They sent him to the Arizona Instructional League over the winter, then let him spend the entire 1984 season at Modesto, again at the single-A level.

There he really began coming on. He led the league with 15 homers and 73 RBIs, and was even playing well in the outfield, picking up 17 assists and starting eight double plays. When 1985 started, the 20-year-old Canseco was playing at the double-A level in Huntsville.

It took just 58 games for another promotion. A .318 average with 25 homers and 80 RBIs in just 58 games at Huntsville convinced them to send José to the A's top triple-A farm club at Tacoma. The kid was really starting to sting the ball on a regular basis.

José did more of the same at Tacoma—a .348 batting average over 60 games, with 11 homers and 47 runs batted in. On September 2, 1985, at the age of 21, he was brought up to the A's. José Canseco was in the major leagues.

He remembers his first at-bat as a pinch hitter against Baltimore that day. "I was so nervous my first time up that my knees were shaking." He struck out on three pitches. In fact, he struck out 12 of his first 24 times at the plate. But in between, he made some noise.

On September 9, he hit his first big-league home run off Jeff Russell of Texas. And then on September 21, batting against Joel Davis of the White Sox, he hit the 40th home run ever to reach the roof of Chicago's Comiskey Park, a tape-measure shot that brought the crowd to its feet. He finished the season with five homers and 13 RBIs in 29 games, and a fine .302 batting average.

That wasn't all. He was named Minor League Player of the Year by *Baseball America,* and his totals for the three teams (Huntsville, Tacoma, and the A's) were a .328 batting average, 41 homers, and 140 runs batted in. It was beginning to look as if the 21-year-old was really ready.

It didn't take the tall, muscular Canseco long to become the sensation of the A's spring training camp at Phoenix in 1986. Teammates, writers, media people began gathering just to watch him take batting practice. The center-field fence at Phoenix Stadium was some 430 feet from home plate and was topped by a 45-foot-high wooden backstop. It was rare for a hitter to clear the backstop, but José Canseco was clearing it routinely during batting practice.

José Canseco watches one of his long home runs fly out of the ballpark. Many consider him the most powerful young slugger in baseball today. *(Courtesy Oakland A's)*

Even the fans were coming out early to watch him take "BP," and he rarely disappointed them.

"He hits a ball and you say there's no way anybody can hit one farther," said A's manager Jackie Moore. "Then he'll hit one even farther. He really puts on a show."

The show would continue right into the season. José was the A's starting left fielder, and in the third game of the season belted his first home run. Ten days later, he smacked another and drove home five runs. On April 21, he slammed a pair against the Angels, and when the month ended he had five homers and 19 RBIs—as well as 26 strikeouts.

One of his homers against the Angels really raised some eyebrows. He smacked it some 430 feet into the upper deck in right field at Anaheim Stadium. And he had hit the opposite-field shot into the teeth of a stiff wind.

"He hits them where I do," said veteran lefty slugger Reggie Jackson, "and he's right-handed."

José continued to hit homers and drive in runs through May. And toward the end of the month he and several other young sluggers were all getting into the news. The Angels' Wally Joyner, another rookie, led the majors with 15 home runs. Canseco had 12, Kirby Puckett of the Twins had 13, and big Pete Incaviglia, a Texas rookie, had 8.

"Canseco can flat-out hit," said the Yanks' Don

Mattingly, considered by many the best all-around hitter in the game.

A's manager Jackie Moore thought the month José spent with the big club the preceding September was a big help. He also said José would be belting them out for a long time.

"I can't say how many he'll hit," Moore said. "But José just crushes the ball and he'll be up among the home-run leaders for years."

He was up among the home-run leaders in early July with 19, and was thought to have a good shot at the rookie record of 38. Like many free-swinging young sluggers, he also blew hot and cold. His batting-practice feats were also becoming legendary, with fans coming out early just to watch him. This may have been part of his problem.

"There are times when I'll catch myself in the cage trying to impress the crowd," José admitted. "I don't think that's doing me much good. It's affecting my mechanics."

One who agreed was hitting coach Bob Watson, who said that José was "taking batting practice for the media. He wants to put on a good show for the people, so he's trying to hit every ball over the roof. He's hurting himself and he can hurt the club."

But José was just a young player flexing his muscles. The slumps ended and he'd hit another hot streak. By the all-star break he had 23 home runs and 78 RBIs. He was really putting together a super rookie season. Everywhere he went there was a media crush that sometimes overwhelmed him. Not used to all the attention, he sometimes appeared aloof and uncomfortable, and the A's decided to make it easier for him.

In each city the team visited, they would hold a short news conference before the first game. That was when José would talk to the media about his great season. It seemed to work better and at least allow him to get away from the constant crush.

He was on the all-star team but didn't get in the game. By August 9, his average was up to .268 and he was still among the leaders in homers and RBIs. But then he fell into a horrendous, 7-for-68 slump that saw his average drop to .241.

It was a struggle the rest of the way. Though he only hit .196 after the all-star break with 10 homers and 39 ribbys, he nevertheless put on a Rookie of the Year performance. His final totals were 33 home runs, fourth best in the American League, and 117 RBIs, second best in the loop. He was also second in the league with 14 game-winning RBIs. That more than compensated for his team-record 175 strikeouts and his .240 batting average.

For the big, free-swinging rookie, the next question was how well he would perform his sophomore season. Would the pitchers find a weakness or would he continue to improve as an all-around hitter? The 1987 A's had a new manager in Tony LaRusso and also a new first baseman, a 6′ 5″

giant named Mark McGwire. McGwire quickly became the José Canseco of 1987, hitting a brace of homers in the early going and capturing much of the media attention.

José wasn't hitting many homers at the outset, but his average was up. The presence of McGwire also shifted some of the media pressure off him and onto the new first baseman. Then in a late June game against the Indians, the A's showed their newfound power potential.

Both Canseco and McGwire hit a pair of homers as the club won, 10–0. They were still in the A.L. West race, and putting on a power parade. McGwire's homers were his 26th and 27th of the season, but José's were just his 13th and 14th. His power was down.

By the all-star break, the big news was Mc-Gwire. He had 33 homers and seemed a cinch to break the rookie mark of 38. There was also talk of his topping the all-time record of 61, held by Roger Maris. When McGwire popped his 37th to tie the American League rookie mark, José contributed a two-run single in the same game.

Then, as the second half of the season wore on, the homers began coming. McGwire slumped in August and it was José Canseco who carried the club. At one point, he even passed McGwire in RBIs. Win or lose, the A's had a one-two punch that really had to be reckoned with, a pair of 23-

year-olds who could really pop the ball. And despite playing second fiddle to McGwire for much of the year, Canseco still elicited raves from many baseball people.

"Canseco is the one man who may break Roger Maris' record," said former Milwaukee manager George Bamberger.

"He has a wicked cut," Boston pitcher Dennis "Oil Can" Boyd said. "I remember him hitting one of my screwballs. He hit it as high as he did hard. He will be legendary."

"You know what I worry about," said batting coach Bob Watson. "I'm afraid he's going to hit the ball so hard up the middle one day that he'll kill the pitcher."

It was a year when the home runs were flying out of ballparks at a record rate. Many people felt the ball had been juiced up. But tests conducted by the Science and Aeronautics Department of the University of Missouri–Rolla showed that the ball was basically the same as it had been. Perhaps it was simply that young sluggers like José, McGwire, and Wally Joyner were just so good that baseball was about to enter a new home-run era.

McGwire came on again in September to complete an amazing rookie year. He finished with a .289 batting average, 49 big home runs, and 118 RBIs. José wasn't far behind. In his second season he walloped another 31 homers, drove home 113 runs, and managed a .257 batting average. He also had 630 at-bats, a very high number for a slugger who usually batted third or fourth in the lineup.

Unfortunately, the A's didn't have the pitching to hold up over the entire year and finished at 81–81. But they weren't far off the pace, finishing just four games behind the division-winning Twins and in third place.

So at the outset of the 1988 season, the A's will have a pair of sluggers with the potential to be one of the most devastating duos ever, back-to-back Rookies of the Year, each with the power to perhaps hit 60 home runs someday. McGwire must still get through his sophomore year and prove that he can prevail now that the pitchers have seen him for a year.

José has put big numbers on the board for two years now, and most baseball people feel he's just scratched the surface. He can still take it up another notch or two, and at 23, he's got more than enough time to do it.

"I just don't want to be known as a one-dimensional ballplayer," José Canseco has said. "I want to hit for high average, steal a base here and there, and do a little of everything."

Then he sounded a warning for the rest of the American League to hear.

"With my ability, the home runs should just come naturally."

Tony Gwynn

In many ways Tony Gwynn is one of the best-kept secrets in baseball. Not to the purists, of course. Baseball people will quickly put the San Diego Padres' young right fielder on the same level with Wade Boggs and Don Mattingly as one of the premier hitters in the game. After all, in just four full seasons in the majors, Gwynn has won a pair of batting titles and has a lifetime mark of .335.

And he seems to be getting better. In 1987 Gwynn led the entire major leagues in hitting with a .370 batting average, accumulating 218 hits along the way. It was the third time in four seasons he has been over the 200-hit mark.

Why, then, is he a secret? Well, Tony Gwynn is one of those quiet guys, a guy who doesn't run his

Tony Gwynn *(Courtesy San Diego Padres)*

mouth in the media, a guy never embroiled in controversy, never at odds with teammates, his manager, or the press. And on top of that, he doesn't hit a lot of home runs.

Yet, in his own way, Tony Gwynn has taken his place among baseball's elite. He's done it quietly, but efficiently, because of an inner drive that moves him to excel.

"I want to be a complete ballplayer," Tony Gwynn has said. "That means being consistent both offensively and defensively. But no matter what happens, I don't think I'll be satisfied. Because once you think you're where you want to be, you're not there anymore."

Tony Gwynn has worked on getting there for a long time. He was born on May 9, 1960, in Los Angeles, but when he was still young his parents moved to nearby Long Beach. That's where Tony first began playing ball with his two brothers, Charles and Chris.

"We would cut up socks that were on the line, put rubber bands around them, and pretend they were baseballs," Tony said. "They were just the size of golf balls, and whoever was pitching would only stand 15 feet away. But I figured if I could hit one of those things, I could hit a baseball."

Eventually, Tony switched to baseballs and continued to hit. By the time he entered San Diego State University he was already an outstanding all-around athlete who came to the school on a basketball scholarship. In fact, he didn't even go out for baseball until his sophomore year.

It was while he was at San Diego State that Tony picked up a habit that continues to this day. Like so many young players, Tony used a big, 34-ounce bat, figuring he could hit the ball farther that way. Then one day he was looking for something in the locker room and happened to pick up a small, 32-inch, 31-ounce bat.

Much to his surprise, the small bat felt comfortable in his hands. He stood up and swung it a few times. Something just felt right. From that day on Tony Gwynn used a bat considered very small by most professional standards. Yet in his final two years at San Diego State, he batted .423 and .416, and you don't argue with numbers like those.

In fact, it was his newfound hitting prowess that led to his being drafted on the third round of the free agent draft in 1981. Though he was also drafted by the NBA's San Diego Clippers the same day, Tony's pick was baseball, and in the summer of 1981 he began his professional career with Walla Walla of the Northwest League.

Early in his minor league career he ran into another future star, Eric Davis, who was just starting out at Eugene. The two young players from the L.A. area talked hitting for a few minutes, then Davis asked to see Gwynn's bat. He couldn't believe the size of it.

"That thing is like a toothpick," said Davis in disbelief.

But the toothpick was getting base hits. All Tony did that first year was lead the Northwest League in hitting with a .331 average in 42 games. And before the season was out he played 23 games at Amarillo, where he compiled an incredible .462 average, getting 42 hits in 91 at-bats—almost one hit for every two attempts!

Though he was just 21 years old, the Padres began thinking Tony was something special. So he opened the 1982 season at Hawaii, in the Pacific Coast League. Padres brass wanted to see what he could do against Triple-A pitching. The answer was plenty.

In 93 games, Tony batted a cool .328, and just past midseason, at the age of 22, he was promoted to the major leagues. He made his big-league debut on July 19, and promptly smacked out a pair of hits against the Phils. Since the Padres played around .500 for most of the year and were out of contention, it was a good time to give a young player like Tony a chance to show his stuff.

And he was showing it pretty well. In August he set a team high for the year by hitting in 15 straight games. But on the 25th, in a game against Pittsburgh, he tried to make a diving catch in the outfield and broke his left wrist. That put him on the shelf for three weeks. He returned in September and showed the kind of hitter he could be by smacking the ball at a .348 clip over the team's final 16 games.

Tony played in 54 games for the Padres in 1982, hitting a respectable .289. Of his 55 hits, 12 were doubles, two went for triples, and he had one home run. But he wasn't supposed to be a power hitter. He felt he had a good chance to win a regular outfield job in '83, and to keep himself sharp he decided to play winter ball in Puerto Rico.

Things went well there until late December. That's when Tony did it again, this time breaking his right wrist. And this time it was worse. He'd be out six months.

"It was the longest six months of my life," Tony said. "I had been looking forward to competing for a starting job in spring training, and instead I was watching from the sidelines."

When he was finally ready, the Padres sent him to Las Vegas to get in shape. He played just 17 games there and was hitting .342 when the Padres recalled him. This time it was for good.

The first month was difficult. In 24 games after his recall, Tony struggled with a .233 mark and he must have wondered whether he really belonged in the majors. But then the hits began to fall in. He was playing every day and really starting to shine.

From August 11 to September 26, Tony hit safely in 39 of the team's 41 games. He put together a 25-game hitting streak at one point that turned out to be the longest in the majors that year. And when the season ended, his batting average was up to .309. The team finished at .500 (81–81) for the second straight year. But it looked as if their new right fielder was a coming star.

There were two important additions to the Padres in 1984. One was the signing of Rich "Goose" Gossage, one of the top relief pitchers in the majors and the bullpen stopper the Padres sorely needed. The other addition wasn't new. It was simply that the Padres would have Tony Gwynn as their regular right fielder from day one.

And Tony produced. Already one of the hardest-working players on the team, he was always out for extra batting practice, using his short, compact swing to spray hits to all fields. He still used his small bat and handled it beautifully. But then again, no one had ever questioned his ability to hit.

With Gossage also contributing heavily, the Padres were battling for the National League West lead. Tony was hitting well over .300, and on June 11 he took over the National League batting lead. In July he smacked the ball at a .389 clip to increase his lead, and at the same time the Padres looked like they might have a good chance to win their division.

And that's just what happened. The Padres

checked in with a 92–70 mark to take the N.L. West. As for Tony Gwynn, he had rapped out 213 hits in 606 trips to the plate to win the batting title with a .351 mark in his first full season in the majors.

Among his hits were 21 doubles, 10 triples, five home runs, and 71 RBIs. He also showed his speed on the bases with 33 steals. It was a fine, all-around year and would see him named to the National League all-star team, as well as finish third in the Most Valuable Player balloting. But there were still the playoffs, and hopefully a trip to the World Series.

The playoffs were still a best-three-of-five series in 1984, and the Padres had to meet the Eastern Division champion Chicago Cubs. The first two games were played at Wrigley Field in Chicago, and when the Cubs won them both by 13–0 and 4–2 scores, it seemed all but over. But the Padres roared back. Playing before sellout crowds at Jack Murphy Stadium, they took game three, 7–1, behind Ed Whitson.

Now it was time for the pivotal fourth game. The excitement was building from the first inning. The Padres jumped off to a 2–0 lead in the third, but the Cubs got three back in the fourth. San Diego tied it again in the fifth, and took a 5–3 lead in the seventh. But when the Cubs tied it again in the eighth, Padres fans began to worry.

It was still a 5–5 game going to the last of the

ninth. And with one out, Tony Gwynn stepped up. He knew his job was to get on base, try to build a run. Facing relief ace Lee Smith, Tony rapped out a solid single. Moments later Steve Garvey smashed a long home run and the Padres had won it, tying the series at two games apiece. Now there was one game left.

This time the Cubs jumped out early, taking a 3–0 lead after two. The Padres were in trouble again. But a pair of San Diego runs in the sixth brought them closer. And in the seventh they rallied again, putting two men on base with Tony Gwynn coming up.

Facing lefty Steve Trout, Tony dug in, got his pitch, and swung. He hit a shot to right center that went between the outfielders. Tony raced to second with a double as the tying and go-ahead runs crossed the plate. It might have been the biggest hit of his life. Before the inning ended the Padres had two more runs for a 6–3 lead. And with Goose Gossage on the mound, the Cubs could do nothing else. San Diego had won the pennant with a miraculous three-game sweep at Jack Murphy Stadium.

Tony had seven hits in 19 at-bats in the playoffs for a .368 average and three runs batted in. And in his first full season in the bigs he was about to play in a World Series. The Padres would be meeting the Detroit Tigers, considered by most observers to be baseball's best team in 1984.

Unfortunately, the World Series proved to be an anticlimax for Tony and the Padres. Detroit won it in five games to become world champs. Tony was just five for 19 in the series, but being there had to be a thrill in itself. In fact, he had had quite an all-around season.

In many ways the 1985 season established Tony as one of the best hitters in the game. Yet it was a year in which he would compile his lowest batting average for a full season. A slow start didn't help, nor did a wrist injury suffered in a home-plate collision at the end of June. That slowed him for nearly a month.

But there were some highlights. On April 28 the Padres were up against the L.A. Dodgers and their ace pitcher Fernando Valenzuela. Valenzuela was hot, not having allowed an earned run in 41⅔ consecutive innings. The game was still scoreless in the ninth inning when Tony came up.

Tony had been having trouble with Valenzuela's southpaw slants but was determined to get something started. He did even better than that. He slammed a pitch deep into the right field pavilion at Dodger Stadium for the only run of the game.

"I think that was the biggest hit I ever got," Tony said afterward. "It's always a thrill to do something like that against a great pitcher like Fernando."

Yet by the end of July Tony's average was below .300, at .296. Now the question was, which way

As a hitter, Tony Gwynn has no weaknesses. In 1987, he led the major leagues with a .370 batting average. *(Courtesy San Diego Padres)*

would it go? And the answer was up. With his wrist healing, he was swinging the bat much better. From August 1 until the end of the year he hit at a .349 clip and finished the season fourth in the National League at .317.

The Padres couldn't repeat as N.L. West champs, but Tony continued his march toward superstardom. He had 197 hits, 3 short of the 200 mark, and led the majors for the second straight year in multiple-hit games with 63. He was also working to become a better outfielder, committing just four errors in 355 chances.

In the offseason Tony continued to work hard. It was, perhaps, his work ethic more than anything else that impressed people. Many players, having achieved a degree of stardom, become complacent. Not Tony Gwynn. He continued to work and worry.

"Tony's very critical of himself," said Padres coach Deacon Jones. "Sometimes I think too much so."

Jones had a point. To hear Tony talk, his hands were too small, his throwing arm weak, his weight too high, he hit into too many double plays, was thrown out stealing too often, and didn't hit with power.

"Well, last year I improved my home runs by one to six," he told a writer before 1986 began. "This year maybe I'll get into double figures. That would be great."

Part of Tony's routine included offseason batting practice sessions with a pitching machine that saw him take some 600 swings a day. He would work on one phase of his batting style, then another. He also decided that at 5′ 11″, 210 pounds, he was playing heavy.

"I've heard all the fat jokes there are," he quipped.

So he went to work on that, running the hills around his San Diego home and even doing some weight work. He also cut down on his eating.

"Funny how I just don't seem to get as hungry anymore," said the former self-confessed junk-food addict. And when he reported to training camp before the 1986 season, he had scaled down to a solid 195 pounds.

"I wasn't sure it was me," Tony joked. "I asked them to double-check if the scales were right."

They were, and so was Tony. When 1986 began, he was right there, pumping out the hits. Of course, the worrier had a bit of a scare when he had just one hit in his first 13 at-bats. But after that, he sailed. On April 27, against the Giants, he had the first two-homer game of his career. In May, he had a .361 average, including a two-out, three-run homer in the ninth inning to win a game against the Mets.

By June he was hitting around the .350 mark and looked to be headed for another bat title. Unfortunately, the team was no longer a contender and had deteriorated noticeably since the pennant-winning year of 1984. The veterans were getting older, some younger players hadn't come through, and a number of trades had more or less backfired. Only Tony Gwynn continued to excel.

Tony finished the year at .329, a close third in the batting race. But he established a number of personal bests, including a career-high 14 home runs. He also swiped a best of 37 bases and won his first Gold Glove as a defensive outfielder.

In addition, he showed amazing consistency by hitting .329 against right-handed pitching and .328 against southpaws. He also amazed people by striking out just 35 times in 701 plate appearances, one of the best ratios in the majors. He was truly one of the all-around stars of the game.

By now, others knew it as well. Veteran star Steve Garvey said Tony was "as complete a player offensively and defensively as you'll find." His manager in 1986, Steve Boros, called him one of the best hitters in the game.

"And by working so hard he's made himself one of the best defensive outfielders around as well," his manager said.

Coach Deacon Jones was another who was full of praise for Tony. "He's just something special, the kind who comes around once every few years."

In 1987 Tony just continued to build his reputation, and he did it while the Padres continued to sink in the West all the way to a basement finish. But for Tony Gwynn, it was simply his best year ever. He made a shambles of the National League batting race, gathering in his second batting crown with a .370 average. That mark was good enough to lead both major leagues.

"For several years now," said one baseball writer, "I thought Wade Boggs of the Red Sox was the only player with a real chance to hit .400. But after this year I think you can add Tony Gwynn to the list."

Tony also led the majors with 218 hits in '87, the third time in four years he had cracked that 200 barrier. But because the Padres had finished dead last, the recognition was again slow in coming. And that's why, in some ways, Tony continues to be one of the best-kept secrets in baseball.

Tony doesn't dwell on this, however, or anything else that's negative. He's a positive person who fully appreciates the things he has achieved and what his baseball skills have allowed him to do.

"I consider myself one of the fortunate ones," he has said. "I'm playing in San Diego, where I went to college and where my parents still live. I have a nice house and two children. And I've been able to give my parents some of the things they've never had despite 40 years of hard work. Because I've been blessed with the ability to hit a baseball, I've got everything I want."

A superstar on the baseball field, Tony Gwynn is also a superstar of a man.

Bret Saberhagen

At some point in most big-league careers a player is called upon to make a comeback. He might have been sidelined by an injury, or simply suffered an inexplicable "off season." And the next year teammates and opponents alike put him under the microscope, waiting to see if he can come back and regain his former skills.

Of course, there is no real way to predict when a player will falter and when he will have to make a comeback, prove himself all over again. Most times, however, it happens later in a player's career, when some think his skills are beginning to diminish.

But what about a player who has to make a comeback at 23? Most players have barely gotten started at that age. In this respect Bret

Bret Saberhagen *(Courtesy Kansas City Royals)*

Saberhagen, the right-handed pitcher of the Kansas City Royals, has been an exception.

Saberhagen had burst on the scene in 1985, a 21-year-old with a blazing fastball, sharp curve, and outstanding control. And all he did that year was win 20 ballgames, a Cy Young Award, a pair of games in the World Series, and take home the MVP prize for the series as he pitched the Royals to the world championship.

He quickly became not only Kansas City's darling, but baseball's newest phenom. And as his agent, Dennis Gilbert, said, "Bret was a guy who couldn't say no. There were times when he would agree to an appearance and have to travel all night to keep the commitment."

Being a 21-year-old World Series hero put extraordinary demands on Bret Saberhagen's time. But for a while he loved it, and it wasn't until spring training for 1986 rolled around that he realized he had overextended himself, that he had spent too much time on the banquet circuit and not enough time preparing to pitch again. When you're 21 years old, you can do things like that.

It took a near-disastrous 1986 season, a season in which his victory total dropped from 20 to 7, to help Bret put his priorities in order. At 23, he was planning a comeback and the stakes were already high.

Bret Saberhagen was born in Chicago Heights, Illinois, on April 11, 1964. A few years later the family moved to the Los Angeles area, and that's where Bret grew up. Like so many other athletes, he took to sports early, and for a time it didn't matter if it was baseball, basketball, or football. He enjoyed them all.

When young Bret was just 11, he became involved with something that could have eventually replaced sports as his number-one love. His father, Bob Saberhagen, was running a private aviation firm and his son was always hanging around, watching the planes come and go. Why not? his father thought, and arranged for his son to take flying lessons. Bret took a few, but after that his father suddenly stopped them. A few years ago he told a reporter why.

"Most people have some fear of flying. It's a healthy attitude, because it makes you cautious," Bob Saberhagen said. "But Bret had no fear. I think he looked at flying the way he looks at hitters today. It was something to beat. And that's bad for a pilot."

So sports remained his top priority, with baseball eventually becoming number one. He went through the Pony League, Colt League, and finally American Legion ball. And he became the top pitcher for Cleveland High School in Reseda, California.

By the time 1982 and his senior year rolled around, young Bret was a star, a reed-thin pitcher who nevertheless had a crackling fastball and a wealth of poise. During the regular season, he compiled a 9–0 record and a minuscule 0.85 earned run average, as well as hitting .362 when he wasn't pitching.

In the title game that year, played at Dodger Stadium, Bret Saberhagen made Los Angeles schoolboy history. He threw a brilliant no-hitter at Palisades High as Cleveland won the championship, 13–0. It was the first no-hitter in Los Angeles prep playoff history, dating back to 1939. And had it not been for an error on the second batter of the game, Saberhagen would have been perfect.

When the 1982 free agent draft rolled around, the Kansas City Royals decided to gamble on the youngster who had just turned 18 a few months earlier. They picked him on the 19th round, hoping he'd sign rather than go to college. Fortunately for the Royals, he did.

According to the Royals, Saberhagen was signed as a shortstop, the position he played when he wasn't on the mound. But when the coaches saw him throw, they knew right away that they wanted him as a pitcher. He was sent to Fort Myers of the Florida State League, where he won his first six decisions, made the all-star team, and had a 10–5 record when he was promoted to Jacksonville, a double-A ballclub.

There, he continued to win, finishing the season at 6–2 with Jacksonville and being named to *Base-*

ball America's First-Year Pro All-Star squad. His combined record as a 19-year-old first-year pro was an impressive 16–7, all games in which he was used strictly as a starter. The question was, could he make the Royals as a 20-year-old in 1984?

The answer was a resounding yes. Bret showed both poise and a live arm, and the Royals kept him as a starter and middle reliever; it wasn't long before he became a valuable member of the K.C. pitching staff. The Royals were in the hunt for a division title all year, so many of Bret's appearances were in pressure-packed situations. And the kid didn't rattle.

His major league debut came on April 4, against the New York Yankees, when he pitched four and two-thirds innings of three-hit relief. And that made him the youngest Royals player ever to appear in a big-league game. He got his first chance to start on April 19, and he threw six innings of one-run ball against Detroit in a 5–2 Kansas City victory that gave him his first big-league win.

After that, he shuffled between starting and the bullpen and played an important role in the Royals' American League Western Division title. He was 6–10 as a starter, going to the hill 18 times in that role. Out of the pen he logged a 4–1 record with a 2.32 ERA in 20 games. That gave him a combined 10–11 mark with a 3.48 ERA in 38 games. One of the highlights was his first shutout, a three-hit whitewash of the Angels on September 24.

If Bret had any regrets after that first year, they were over the designated hitter rule in the American League.

"I was always real excited about the idea of hitting in the major leagues," said Bret. "There were times when I'd talk more about hitting than pitching."

Though the Royals were beaten quite handily by the Detroit Tigers in the American League play-offs, Bret pitched impressively in his one start. He threw eight innings in game two and gave up just two runs, though the Tigers won it in 11 innings, 5–3. Still, Bret had become the youngest pitcher ever to start an American League Championship Series game.

The experience he gained pitching in playoff action would help him a lot sooner than even he imagined. He was still a few days away from his 21st birthday when 1985 began, but his spring training performance earned him a spot in the K.C. starting rotation. And he pitched well right from the start of the season.

He showed just how dominant he could be on May 17, when he threw a brilliant, two-hit shutout against the Brewers. In four July starts he went 30⅔ innings without walking a single batter.

Against Oakland on September 14, he set a career high of 12 strikeouts in a 2–1 complete-game victory.

As the season wore on the Royals began to look as if they would take another division title. And Bret Saberhagen, gaining confidence, was quickly becoming the ace of the staff. As K.C. drove toward a title, Saberhagen spearheaded the move by winning seven consecutive starts between July 23 and September 2. He was headed toward a possible 20-win season, and for the first time there was talk of the youngster having a shot at the coveted Cy Young Award.

It was Bret's strong finish as much as anything else that helped the Royals win another American League West title. Mixing a 90-plus-mile-per-hour fastball with a curve and a newly acquired change-up, he baffled American League hitters to the tune of 10 wins in his final 11 decisions. The Royals took the division, and young Bret Saberhagen had become the toast of the league.

He finished the 1985 season with a remarkable 20–6 record, becoming the fifth-youngest pitcher in baseball history to win 20 games. He had 10 complete games, fanned 158 hitters in 235 innings, and walked just 38. His earned run average was a fine 2.87.

In the playoffs, the Royals faced the surprising Toronto Blue Jays, a team that had just taken its first-ever American League East title. As things turned out, the Royals came back from a 3–1 deficit to win the series in seven exciting games. As for their young ace, however—well, Bret must have thought the Blue Jays were using him for target practice.

He started game three and early on was hit on the foot by a line drive and felled. Though he stayed in the game, he was socked for five runs and nine hits in just four and a third innings. But he wouldn't blame the line drive.

"I wasn't busting them enough inside," he simply said.

But he got another chance in the crucial seventh and deciding game. This time he had his good stuff, but after pitching three scoreless innings, he was hit on his pitching hand by a line drive. He left the game, but fortunately the Royals came on to win it. They were American League champs and heading for a World Series showdown with the St. Louis Cardinals.

When the Redbirds won the first two games in Kansas City, the second with a dramatic, four-run ninth inning, most observers thought the series was done. After all, the Cards were heading home with all the momentum going their way. But in game three the Royals had Bret Saberhagen waiting for them.

Determined to make up for his no-decisions in the playoffs, Saberhagen went to work. He did so knowing that his wife, Janeane, was expecting a baby any day back in Kansas City. And for a 21-year-old, he went to work with a very laid-back attitude.

"What we are is confident and relaxed," he told reporters before the game.

That he was. On the mound he stopped the Cardinals on just six hits while striking out eight, winning the game, 6–1, as he went the distance and brought the Royals their first win in three games. But when Cardinal ace John Tudor blanked the Royals in game four, K.C. found itself behind, 3–1, just as it had been against Toronto. Could they come back a second time?

Incredibly, they won games five and six, forcing the series to a seventh game. And their pitcher would be none other than Bret Saberhagen. Bret would be starting the biggest game of his life just 36 hours after rushing back to Kansas City to witness the birth of his son, Drew William. So it was a storybook scenario, as Saberhagen would be facing Cardinal ace Tudor, who had already beaten the Royals twice.

Bret walked out to the mound in Kansas City, a brand-new father and the youngest pitcher ever to start the seventh game of a World Series. Amazingly, he didn't seem nervous at all. Later he would say that his control had never been better than it was that day.

"Every time I missed, it was high or low, or

On the mound, Bret Saberhagen is an intense competitor who hates to lose. *(Courtesy Kansas City Royals)*

maybe wide," he explained. "But it was never into the middle of the plate."

Translated, that meant Saberhagen had his good stuff, and he went about the business of dispatching Redbirds. And while he was throwing goose eggs at the Cards, the Royals were battering John Tudor and the Cardinal relievers. When the smoke cleared, the Royals had won the game, 11–0, as Bret Saberhagen twirled a five-hit shutout. Kansas City had won the World Series, and Saberhagen had become the youngest MVP in series history.

"What more can I ask for?" he crowed afterward. "It's like the world's at my feet."

It was true. And when he was named winner of the Cy Young Award as the best pitcher in the American League a short time later, he was in demand everywhere. The offseason became a whirlwind tour. Appearances on the "Today" show, on "Good Morning America," then off to California for "The Tonight Show." There were banquets, celebrity golf tournaments, and trips back home to visit wife and child. It was an exhausting schedule, even for a 21-year-old.

And when the Royals raised his salary for 1986 from $100,000 to $925,000, it did seem, indeed, that the world was at his feet. Then came spring training.

Things began going wrong right away. The first

week his right foot began hurting. After that it was the flu. Then his shoulder began to ache. By the time spring training ended, he only had some 12 innings under his belt. Bad luck? Perhaps. But even Saberhagen himself soon realized that the offseason and all its activities had been too much.

"I guess I had to learn the hard way," he said. "I just exhausted myself mentally and physically. I looked at everything as a chance to make a lot of money. But I later realized that if I stayed healthy and had another real good year, I could have made three or four times as much."

Because he didn't pitch much in the spring, he was scratched as the opening-day starter. But when he finally got back in action, there were some signs of the old Saberhagen. In his second start of the year at Boston on April 16, he pitched a brilliant, two-hit shutout, striking out six. But that would be his best game of the season. After that, things went downhill.

By the all-star break he was a 4–10 pitcher and he was struggling. There were few signs of the dominant hurler of '85. Now, at the age of 22, Bret Saberhagen was just another pitcher, and a mediocre one at that. And things didn't get better. In August he went on the disabled list with a bum shoulder and didn't pitch again until September 6.

"It was extremely frustrating," he said. "I was hurting, but some people didn't think so. They thought I wasn't taking the game seriously. But the team was out of it and I didn't want to mess with my career."

He made three starts in September, but won only one game after July. His final record was a disappointing 7–12, with a 4.15 earned run average. There would be no heroics in 1985.

Now there was really something to prove—to himself, his teammates, and the fans. The Royals were a team in transition, and were also under a cloud of tragedy. Their popular manager, Dick Howser, was stricken with brain cancer during the 1986 season and would live only another year. Billy Gardner replaced him and tried to regroup the ballclub.

As for Bret, he went about regrouping himself. He packed up his family and went to live with his in-laws in the warmth of California during the offseason. There, he began throwing six days a week and refused to make any public appearances after Christmas. This time, when spring training rolled around, he was ready.

"I came to Florida bigger and in better shape than ever before," he said. "My arm was already strong, and by the time we went north I knew I was back."

Others agreed. Royals catcher Jamie Quirk was one of the first to see the difference. "Bret came back better than '85," Quirk said. "He was throwing much harder and just dominating people the way Roger Clemens did for the Red Sox. And his confidence was back."

On April 10 Bret held the hard-hitting Yankees hitless into the eighth and finished with a two-hitter. On May 9 he went into the seventh inning at Cleveland with a perfect game and wound up with another shutout. He was the Royals' stopper once again, with five of his first seven victories following K.C. defeats.

He was off to a phenomenal start and helping to keep the Royals in the thick of the A.L. West race. In late June the team was shattered by news of former manager Dick Howser's death. Five hours later, Bret went to the mound and defeated the A's to run his season's record to an amazing 12–1.

"Before the game, I was going out there thinking, maybe this one is for him," Saberhagen said. "I don't know if the other guys in here were thinking that or not. But we just went out to play a good game."

By the all-star break, Bret Saberhagen had the best record in the major leagues, a 15–3 log with a league-leading 2.47 ERA. He also had 11 complete games. Needless to say, he got the starting nod against the National League.

The second half was something less. The Royals, as a team, went downhill and slowly dropped out of the race. There was another managerial change, and the team just couldn't seem to put it together. Perhaps this affected Bret's performance; certainly he just wasn't the same pitcher over the final two months. He still had his good stuff, but didn't always have the support. But all things considered, it was still a fine season.

He finished the year with an 18–10 record, throwing a career-high 257 innings. He also had a high of 163 strikeouts and walked only 53. His earned run average was 3.36, fourth best among the league's starting pitchers. In view of what had happened the year before, it was a great comeback.

"The last two seasons have allowed me to think about what it takes to stay on top once you're there," he said. "I've been up there, and then I was down. And at 22, I had to figure how to get back up there again."

Bret will only be 24 years old in 1988, and much of his pitching life is still in front of him. With his natural ability, he still has a chance to be one of the game's best for many years to come. And because he had to learn such a difficult lesson early in his career, the odds are that he will now work to fulfill every bit of his great potential, and to remain one of the hot new stars of the game.

About the Author

BILL GUTMAN has been an avid
sports fan ever since he can remember.
A freelance writer for sixteen years, he
has done profiles and bios of many of
today's sports heroes. Although Mr.
Gutman likes all sports, he has written
mostly about baseball and football. Currently, he lives in Poughquag, New
York, with his wife, two step-children,
and a variety of pets. He is also the
author of Archway's *Sports Illustrated*
series.